APEX

MM SPORTS ROMANCE

VICTORIA DENAULT

For 'my kids' Aimee and Adam

FASTER Series

Welcome to our *FASTER* world. **Everything**, including characters, teams, and locations, is ***fictional***. We wanted to create our own world, so we ***intentionally*** departed from real-world racing schedules, track layouts, race lengths, rules, and so on. Our characters are **not** based on real drivers. We're also aware that Formula One uses British spelling for things like "tyres" and "chequered" flag, and we do not. To make it easier to follow, we're supplying a list of our teams and our race schedule on the following pages. Happy reading!

LIGHTHOUSE RACING

Cristian Rivera

Samantha Stevens

SC RACING

Jasper Nord

Raj Singh

LARUE MOTORSPORTS

Rene Savard

Grady Lewis

MAYFLOWER RACING

Gabriel Allard

Sterling Samuels

ARETE GRAND PRIX

Yanni Castellanos

Lionel Hartt

MIRABELLA RACING

Billy James

Lucia Castera

AND MORE....

THE RACE SCHEDULE

BAHRAIN
ABU DHABI
AZERBAIJAN
HUNGARY
AUSTRIA
BELGIUM
NETHERLANDS
MONACO
AUSTIN
MEXICO
BRAZIL
AUSTRALIA
JAPAN
BREAK
ITALY
MONTREAL
MIAMI
LAS VEGAS
FRANCE
SINGAPORE

THERE ARE OTHER RACES NOT LISTED

Zack and Bob Johnson are the business partners I've never wanted. Loud, arrogant, rude, brash Americans. Yeah, I know. I sound like a snotty Frenchman. I fucking am. A Parisienne through and through, which is the worst kind of Frenchman, if you go by stereotypes. But I'm also a worldly business owner who built a fashion empire from the ground up. I've seen enough of life to know stereotypes are bullshit.

There are kind, polite Frenchmen. Just like there are good, refined American business owners. People with manners and ethics and morals. But the Johnsons... just aren't that. Their dad made the family rich with a fast food joint that took off in the sixties in Texas and grew across the United States, becoming a multi-million dollar franchise by the mid-seventies. The company moved into grocery stores with a frozen food division and into backyards with grilling equipment, too. It wasn't until Daddy Johnson started having health issues ten years ago, and a battle ensued for C.E.O. that would have rivaled the best episode of *Succession*, that the company diversified into auto racing. Because the sons wanted it.

And that's how I'm here, in hot and humid Houston, Texas, sitting across an obscenely large conference table from Zack Johnson and his brother Bob. Because they needed millions, and I had millions, and I wanted to invest in a racing team. Not for me, but for my son.

Bob clears his throat, making this thick, wet sound that makes me want to shudder. "I don't know how this will work now."

"The same way it was working last week," I reply, trying not to sound as annoyed as I am. Luckily my thick French accent when I speak English always makes me sound slightly annoyed, so he isn't going to notice a difference. "Nothing has changed."

"We're a family-run business. We have... strong Christian values and your son... I mean, first the paternity issue..."

"Two different paternity tests proved he wasn't the father," I remind Zack.

"And now... the accusation by a member of your staff," Zack shoots back. Like I'm a fool who forgot.

"Accused is not convicted. And it's a *former* member of my staff," I say because facts are key here. "She was fired weeks before she made the accusation."

"It's an image issue for the entire team *if* he continues to drive for us," Bob adds.

"He *is* driving for you," I reply, again, cooler than a cucumber because regardless of this woman's lies, I hold the cards in this business relationship. "You've had image issues before, so this isn't new. Remember when everyone was talking about how you lost so much money in the E. coli outbreak settlement at your restaurants that you weren't going to have enough money to keep the Formula One team going? You survived that crisis by taking my money, which guaranteed my son a seat on your team."

"Yes but... PR nightmares cost more money." Bob pulls off his hat, a cowboy hat, of course, and places it on the table. Then he takes one of his meaty hands and wipes away the sweat plastering what's left of his fine hair to his oddly squarish head. Look, I'm usually not this judgmental or crass about people's looks, but I'm fighting for my son. His career and his reputation. I'm a single dad, by choice, and the biggest baddest mama bear you've ever seen. Proud of it.

"I'll handle his PR," I offer. "On my dime. On top of the money I've already invested."

Zack glances at Bob. "He just needs to clean up. Settle down. Last night he was out at some bar, drunk, with an Influencer or some such nonsense. The pictures in the papers make him look...."

"Like he isn't taking this—us, our brand, and his job with us —seriously," Bob finishes for his brother.

"I'll hire the best public relations, just like I got him the best lawyer for this false accusation," I fold my arms over my chest, which is covered in one of my own designer suits. "I. Will. Handle. It."

Bob still looks leery but Zack doesn't. At least not as much as he did. I lean forward and decide to gently explain to these men how it's going to go. Because they honestly don't have a choice. "I am not just saying this as a blind-eyed parent. Gabriel's innocence will be proven in time. But the simple fact is you have two options. Stay the course, with Allard Couture money bankrolling this season and my son as your second driver, or drop him and repay me."

"There's nothing in our contract that says if we drop Gabriel we have to repay you," Bob says, his voice now too growly for my liking. "You wanted it that way."

I did. Because I didn't want Gabriel to be saddled with

being called a pay driver, which is someone who only gets a seat on a team because he's bringing bank, not because he knows how to drive and win. But my rightfully talented son has been labeled it anyway so I might as well play the card. This fucking sport... *merde.*

I stand, done with this meeting. "But there is also no morality clause in that contract so if you fire him for something that hasn't been proven, we *will* sue and I *will* get my money back. And then I'll just buy the entire team from you when you can't afford to keep it going. You seem to forget the four sponsors that came on board when our deal was announced. Because of me."

"We lost two different ones when the most recent scandal broke about Gabe," Zack says.

"I'll find you more," I throw out with confidence because I fucking will. You watch.

The two men exchange glances again. Zack turns his ruddy face to me. "Can we get that in writing?"

"No. Because you don't need it in writing because it's a favor," I reply. "I don't owe you this. I gave you your options. Keep him, and my money, or deal with the legal hellfire I will rain down on you. You can call my assistant with your decision. Or email me. *Bonne journée.*"

I walk out of the boardroom and don't stop walking until I'm out of the building. Henri is behind me the entire time. Like my shadow, silent but always there. His technical title is Director of Global Affairs, but he's just an executive assistant with a marketing degree. But he's efficient, smart, and puts up with my type-A personality.

I resist the urge to curse the Texans. I remind myself of all the fine, charming American men I've dated. And that this isn't about their nationality. This team *is* a good fit for Gabriel, even though it's owned by cretins.

I yank my cell phone from the pocket of my pants before I get into the waiting SUV, which thankfully has tinted windows and the AC already blasting. I am not a fan of air-conditioning normally, but in Texas, it's required. I punch Gabriel's number on my cell. My son, *mon coeur*, sends me to voicemail. I end the call. No point in leaving yet another message. He hasn't responded to the last six. I swear under my breath.

"You know it's going to make it very hard to save his reputation and clean up his image if he won't even take your calls," Damien murmurs quietly like his tone can soften the blow of that blunt statement. It can't. Damien is the head of my legal team. I had him waiting in the car in case things got ugly. He's working in tandem with Henri on Gabriel's latest image issue.

"He will fall in line. He knows what's at stake," I promise. I truly believe that too. Just like I believe Damien is the right person for this job. Well, one of them. "Now who is going to back you up on this?"

"This guy is my recommendation," Henri says and turns his phone screen to face me. "He applied with our Marketing and Public Relations department last month, and we didn't hire him because he was ridiculously overqualified for the job, but I kept his resume. He used to own his own firm. Bullet Proof PR."

I lift my eyebrows. "That firm out of New Zealand? The one that worked with—"

"Every actor with a successful comeback story. Every rock star with a successful rebirth. Every brand with a successful rebrand. Yeah. He owned that firm. And it was Australian. *He* is Australian."

I look at the headshot on the web page Damien is showing me. The guy looks to be a little older than Gabriel, but not much. He's clean-cut with an intelligent glint in his eye. Axel Walsh. "Damien, your thoughts?"

"He's a fit. He needs the money if he's applying for entry-level jobs," Damien replies. "He doesn't have a record. I checked. And he's openly gay."

"He sounds perfect. So what happened to his company? Did he sell?"

"His business partner left, took the clients. It was ugly," Henri informs me. "I'm not sure why the clients willingly left, but here is something I do know — he is good friends with Billy James. So he knows the sport, somewhat."

Billy James is a driver on a European team called Mirabella Racing. Billy and the rookie Grady Lewis on the Larue team are the only drivers who are friends with Gabriel. Well, friends might be a stretch, but I've seen them talking to him. Willingly.

"Interesting..." I stare out the window as the dirty streets and gleaming towers blur by. "Set up a meeting with him for me, please. As soon as possible."

"Already done. He's meeting us at the Paris office tomorrow at ten," Henri says, closing his laptop.

"And you still think the relationship thing is how we should go?" I question because I am second-guessing everything about this now.

"Yeah. I'm positive it's the right path," Henri replies confidently.

"Axel might have some ideas of his own we haven't yet considered," Damien adds. "And that's the type of guy we need. Someone who knows the game and can think on his feet. I like your son, Louis, but he is a wild card."

"I will not argue there," I confess. Gabriel's passion is one of my favorite things about him, but it tends to make him moody and unpredictable.

"But I'm confident if we get this Walsh guy on board, he'll help this whole thing calm down quicker than anyone else. Maybe even quicker than Henri."

"Pft!" Henri makes the quintessential sound of a pissed-off Frenchman.

I smile for the first time since Gabriel's troubles began. Because I feel like there might be a light at the end of the tunnel that isn't an oncoming train. And it's Axel Walsh.

1 / AXEL

THIS IS MY BREAK. The miracle I've been looking for. The light at the end of a very long tunnel. A tunnel I threw myself in. Because I'm an idiot who falls for shady, selfish assholes. I shake off that last thought and play with my cufflinks for the millionth time.

I want to check the time but I don't wear a watch and I'm scared that if I pull out my phone, they'll walk in at that exact moment and I'll look like an asshole. So I twist my cufflink instead and try to stay calm. I don't know what job they're offering me but unless it's head clothing designer or bathing suit runway model, I am confident I'm qualified.

I built a PR company from the ground up. I went from making seventeen thousand my first year to one point four million last year. I did that. No matter what Eric tells people, I know it was all me. And yeah, Allard Couture is an already established, billion-dollar mega-brand, but I can put out mega-fires.

The door to the room opens and a tall, slender man in an Allard suit walks in with a cool smile. "Sorry to keep you waiting Mr. Walsh."

I stand and lean forward to shake his hand across the table as a shorter, rounder man in a different Allard suit walks in. "Hi. Damien Fischer. I'm head of legal."

"Oh and I'm Henri Boutin," the first guy, whose voice I recognize as the one who arranged the interview, says. "And this is Louis Allard."

Before I can register what's happening the man who built the company saunters into the room, closing the door behind him. He turns and greets me with a warm, but brief smile and extends his hand. "*Bonjour*. I'm Louis. Please have a seat."

I am going to faint. Louis Allard is interviewing me? It's like applying for a job at the White House and having the President interview you. I am not prepared. And I am most certainly not prepared for the next thing that happens.

"So listen, Axel," Damien says, dropping his elbows onto the table. "We have a unique situation. And you might be the right fit."

And then, Damien the lawyer, asks me to sign a non-disclosure form. Which I do without even reading because I know how this business works. I have to pretend this never happened, this meeting, or I get sued. Fine. But why? Why is there an NDA at a job interview?

My question gets answered as Damien takes the signed form back and launches into a story I've heard at least fifty times before. Rich guy gets accused of something inappropriate by a woman. Rich man denies wrongdoing. Woman sues. Only the name in this story is one I know. Gabriel Allard. Son of the man sitting across from me, an elite race car driver and also... a guy I once kissed.

"So... we've got a plan. Several actually," Henri says and now it's his turn to slide a file folder my way. "But we aren't one hundred percent on any of them."

I've seen this before. It's a strategy package. This one has three different tactics outlined. I read them as quickly as possible. It's nerve-wracking and I can't stop thinking about the way Louis Allard is just sitting there silently, hands folded, eyes never leaving me, like he's assessing me for some test I don't know I'm taking. I let my mind assess the ideas and make a mental list of hits and misses, which is essentially like a pros and cons list.

"So if you're asking my opinion, with the basic amount of information I have," I pause. "I would go with strategy one."

"The fake relationship," Damien reaffirms and gets a big grin on his face when I nod.

I honestly don't like the idea of Gabriel, the best kiss of my life, fake dating someone but it's been years, and it's not like I pined for him. I didn't. I was embroiled in a long, horrible relationship, and Gabriel... well I've seen his face in tabloids and on gossip sites with various women hanging off him. And there *was* the pregnancy scandal a couple months ago.

I hadn't been following Gabriel Allard's life (I mean sure maybe a quick Google search every now and then), but my best friend is also an F1 driver and I listen when he talks about work. Also, the media kind of blew that paternity thing right up. It was everywhere. It isn't every day a fashion mogul's only child is accused of fathering a child with a one-night stand.

"Mr. Walsh?" Louis Allard says firmly.

Oh my God, I just spaced out in the middle of the biggest interview of my life. Was Eric right? Am I not cut out for this anymore? I sit straighter and refocus.

"Fake dating has so many advantages here," I explain confidently. "One, it diverts public interest from the woman in question to the new one. Two, it shows a human side to the accused, which is the perfect way to combat the negative press that is sure to be written. Three, the public loves a good love story, and they see people in love as better, kinder, and more likely to be innocent than perpetually single people. It's an absolute flaw in the human brain, but it's true. So the caveat here is you need to make sure both the client and the person you hire for the role of significant other are on board. Have chemistry. And PDA is required."

Well, that was quite the soliloquy. I feel my face start to heat. I mean, I know that everything I said is true, but I still feel a swell of panic because all three of these men are not just looking at me, but examining me. I feel like I'm missing something big. "Is the job I'm here for related to this problem? Because I thought I was here for an Allard Couture position."

"It is in fact related to this issue," Damien confirms.

All the hope and positive energy I've been feeling since I got the call from Henri fizzles in my chest like a defective firework. I can't work with Gabriel Allard. And I can't tell them why. I haven't told anyone about that night. Not even Billy. And I don't intend to tell anyone, ever. "What could I possibly add to the situation? You seem to have it under control. I mean, you've got a solid plan to implement."

They stop looking at me and start looking at each other. My anxiety ratchets up as I try to figure out what the absolute fuck is going on here. Louis Allard leans forward, his eyes, which are the color of melted caramel, hold mine. "I have two more questions for you. What happened to your company? Why are you here, interviewing with us, when you created and ran one of the most successful PR companies in Australia?"

Shit. I blink. Look away and then look back. I have a bucket of canned responses I've been practicing. I didn't like the administrative work that comes with running a company. I needed a new challenge. I wanted more global work. I decided to move on before burnout happened. The problem with standard, canned responses is that people like Louis Allard know what they are. So I do the stupidest thing possible and tell him the truth. "My accounts manager decided to leave the company and took the top ten percent of my clients with him."

Mr. Allard doesn't look shocked. "And you couldn't make it work with the other ninety percent?"

"I could have. But the top ten were seventy-five percent of my revenue." I feel my palms get moist, so I press them into my pant legs under the table. "The accounts manager also tried to muddy my name. He made some massive errors in campaigns and blamed me for it to the clients. So I would have had to rebuild more than just fiscally, and I wasn't in the headspace to do that."

"Why not?"

"Because I was also going through a break-up from a six-year relationship," I admit. "With my former account manager."

Now Louis Allard looks shocked. But the expression moves quickly off his face. He's not one to let things throw him off. He wouldn't be as successful as he is if he was. I sigh and start to stand up, figuring we're done here. I mean who is going to hire a guy who tanked his own company by dating the wrong guy. But Louis raises one single hand in the air. A finger actually. I notice the tattoo on his wrist as his sleeve slips down. A set of Roman numerals. I'm shocked someone of his age and stature has a tattoo. He's still of the generation that kind of looks down on them. But again, that shows his maverick attitude. He wouldn't be where he is if he toed the line either.

Mr. Allard motions for me to sit down. I hesitate. He gives me a hint of a smile. "I'm still looking for your services, Mr. Walsh so unless you aren't interested in a position with Allard Couture, you should stay."

I sit. Mr. Allard looks at Henri and Damien. They turn back to me. "So you asked how you can help in this strategy. Well, we need a person who can play the role of partner to Gabriel. And we want it to be you."

Me? Fake date Gabriel Allard. The model handsome, sexy as hell, wild child who kissed me like it was the last thing he would ever do? The guy who is larger than life, passionate, bold, impetuous, and everything I am not and also not comfortable being around? I give them the only answer I can. "No."

2 / AXEL

"But if you said no, then why are you standing here with me right now?" Billy James asks me, his dirty blond eyebrows raised high as he swirls the whiskey in his tumbler and leans back against the oak bar we're standing next to.

"Because they wouldn't take no for an answer," I reply and bring my own whiskey to my lips. "But as for why we are here, in this vortex of hell known as a karaoke bar, well you'll have to explain that to me. You're the one who picked it."

"It's drag queen karaoke. Hosted by Montreal's number one drag queen and the room is filled with hot gay men, mate," Billy says, tipping his head toward the crowded tables peppered throughout the room, all facing the stage in front of us, waiting for Mademoiselle Kitara L'amour to start the show. "And you need to get laid, my friend."

"I am *not* getting laid tonight," I retort sharply.

A cute stocky brunette guy grabbing two beer bottles from the bartender to my left turns to me and gives me a once over. "Not with that attitude you're not."

And then he walks away. Billy, of course, bursts out laughing as I turn my usual fifty shades of red. The one thing I have never been able to control is the temperature of my face. Oh hell, if I'm honest it's not the only thing I can't control. I huff out a breath. "You're a dick, Billy."

"Yeah. I know." He winks. "Now let's get back to why you are here, in Montreal, with me at the Grand Prix if you turned down the job with Allard."

"Because when I explained to them that I didn't want to fake date their race car driving problem child, my excuse was that I was looking for full-time work and this would be a stop-gap solution that would be beneficial monetarily but that it wasn't even something I could put on my resume," I reply and my brain fills with memories of being in that boardroom in Paris. How Mr. Allard and the others really seemed to be understanding my rationale. "And that's when they said they'd pay me double for the time I was working with Gabriel and give me a title at Mayflower. Public Relations consultant. And said I would be given a full-time position in Allard Couture immediately after completion of this job."

"Wow. Doing what?"

"Director of Public Relations for their entire United Kingdom division," I reply. It's a dream position and not one someone like me can walk into easily, even with my previous experience. So it's truly not something I can give up. I don't tell Billy this but I'm sure he gets it. He knows I'm not one to put myself in uncomfortable or risky situations without a valid reason. And fake dating anyone, especially Gabriel, is all of that.

"Well, selfishly, I'm looking forward to having you around, Axe," Billy says. "And I'm more than a little intrigued at how this will play out."

"That reminds me, I need to make you sign an NDA," I mutter and pull my phone out of my pocket to add it to the digital to-do list I keep.

Billy laughs. "I'll sign anything but you know you can trust me."

"I know. It's just... due diligence," I reply and tuck my phone back into my back pocket. I do trust Billy. But I trusted Eric too. Of course, Billy is very different from Eric. Billy has been my best friend since I was a kid, and he's never been anything *more* than a friend. He's as straight as an arrow and always has been and I have never been attracted to him anyway, despite his classic good looks.

We both sip our whiskey in silence and then Billy says, with a seriousness to his voice that is often lacking, "You don't get what a bitch of a job you just signed up for."

"I've done PR for half a decade. I know what I'm doing."

"Now you're in the F1 world, Axe. The days are never-ending. The time off seems lengthy on paper, with two or three weeks between a couple of races, but jet lag eats that up. And when there aren't races there are promotional shoots, interviews, sponsorship obligations. You'll be lucky to sleep in your own bed once a month for the next eight." Billy looks tired just talking about it. But I know he loves it. It's in his blood. His dad was a driver too. Although his career, and life, ended in a crash. I thank the stars every time a season ends and Billy is still with us.

A very attractive drag queen saunters onto the stage and the crowd erupts in cheers and hoots. After a few jokes and kicking off the night with the first song—"I Will Survive"—Mademoiselle L'Amour reaches into a big jar of names and pulls out the first singer of the evening.

"Mr. Cole Trickle will sing 'Dirty Laundry' by Don Henley!"

Everyone claps and there's movement from a table near the front. Billy makes a face. "Cole Trickle? That's the name of Tom Cruise's character in *Days of Thunder*."

"Days of what?" I ask, leaning into him because it's hard to hear with the clapping and hooting.

"It's a movie about racing. NASCAR," Billy shouts back over the noise.

"Ah the lesser sport," I reply and wink because Billy has been drilling the difference between NASCAR and F1 into my head since we met. He grins at me and shoves my shoulder before his eyes move to the stage and his expression goes completely blank.

"What?"

"I should have known..." Billy laughs and points with his whiskey glass. "Your assignment is about to sing."

My eyes fly to the front of the room and I couldn't be more shocked if a kangaroo reared up and box kicked me in the chest. Gabriel Allard is standing in the middle of the stage, his strong, handsome profile gleaming in the lights as he watches Mademoiselle L'Amour sashay off stage.

He turns forward and grabs the microphone. The full weight of his good looks washes over me. Nothing has changed since the first time I saw him five years ago. He's still tall, for an F1 driver. His hair is still shaggy sandy brown. The kind of shag that is purposeful and looks both unkempt and strategically placed at the same time. His shoulders are still broad, his neck still a goddamn tree trunk. His eyes are still a deep obscenely pretty blue... although they're currently a little unfocused and glassy.

"He's drunk."

"We're in a bar, Axe. Not an uncommon characteristic," Billy reminds me.

"Why is he here, though?" I ask. "He should be laying low. A groping accusation is serious."

"He probably needs some stress relief." Billy shrugs and

scratches the back of his blond head. "Probably also wants to do what you won't. Get laid."

"He needs a one-night stand less than I do," I reply with a tired sigh. "Have they not informed him of the PR plan?"

"This song is for all the fucking haters. I'd list them but we would be here all night," Gabriel says into the microphone and then the music starts.

I thought my first official day of work was tomorrow. But it starts right now because I'm going to have to make sure that this stupid rock star moment is the only stupid thing Gabriel Allard does tonight. I hiss out a couple swear words under my breath, which seems to amuse Billy because he grins as he finishes his whiskey.

"Not a bad voice," Billy says, leaning into me.

I shake my head. Yeah, Gabriel sounds great, but I'm more concerned about his song choice. "Dirty Laundry" is a lesser-known eighties song written by the guy from the Eagles about how slimy journalism has become. The absolute worst choice for a guy who needs to get the press on his side.

My work brain kicks in and I scan the crowd for people who might be recording this. I don't see any, but that doesn't mean it's not happening. Fuck. Thankfully he gets bored and wanders off stage before the song ends. Right into the arms of a guy who hugs him a little too hard and a little too long. They sit beside each other and the dude wraps his arm around the back of Gabriel's chair. If Billy's right and Gabriel is also here to get laid, he's got someone willing to volunteer as tribute, obviously.

Billy smiles his typical shit-stirring smile. "You two could fuck each other. Two birds. One stone. Problem solved. Also, will totally help sell the relationship."

I've known Billy James since we were twelve. His family moved into the house next door to mine. But that isn't how we met because the house next door to mine was two and a half kilometers away. I grew up on a compound in Byron Bay. A sprawling main house with two guest houses, a pool twice the size of an Olympic one, and breathtaking views of the sea. Billy's place was equally impressive. But due to the size of both properties, he lived there almost three months before we came face-to-face. We met at the posh private school everyone in that neighborhood went to. Outside the Dean's office. I was there to get my schedule. He was there because he'd already been in a fight. Billy has been a troublemaker since day one and I love that for him. It works. But not for me. I glare at Billy and he bursts out laughing.

"Don't get your knickers in a knot, mate," he says and slaps my shoulder. "I know you don't mix business and pleasure."

"I did. Eric. And look how that turned out."

"There was nothing pleasurable about that tosser," Billy retorts and makes a face at the mention of my ex who he never liked. "Good riddance to bad rubbish."

I keep my eyes on Gabriel who is doing nothing of note, thankfully. His friend is whispering something in his ear and rubbing his back in tiny circles with his tiny hand. Yeah, I'm petty. Sue me.

"So does he know it's you?"

"I don't think he knows about the plan at all," I reply. "We have a meeting tomorrow. It was one stupid kiss and he probably doesn't even remember."

I finally broke down and told Billy about that fateful kiss when I told him I accepted the job at Mayflower. He is way more amused by the revelation than I would like. It's his fault it even happened. He was the one who dragged me to that party and then disappeared.

"I guess we'll find out soon enough," Billy chuckles again. Sometimes my best friend is a pain in my ass.

"Did you know he was going to be here?"

"No. Honest to God." Billy lifts his hands up. "Total coincidence. I just brought you here for a random hook-up to take the edge off your mood, which has been morose as hell since... well the whole company thing."

Billy turns and drops his empty whiskey glass on the bar top and clasps my shoulder. "Now I'm going to take a piss and when I return I expect a fresh drink and a list of potential one-night stands you're interested in."

"Sex isn't the answer," I tell him.

"Sex is always the answer." Billy winks and disappears into the crowd.

I sigh and my eyes move through the crowd to find Gabriel Allard again. He's standing now, in front of his table, while a woman belts out off-key Carrie Underwood on the stage. The guy who is clearly obsessed with him is also standing, his hands on Gabriel's biceps as Gabriel talks to him.

His clingy friend's pupils are so big I can see them from here. Higher than a kite. God, I hope Gabriel isn't high too. I'm not against recreational drug use but it will look bad if someone sees him high. Not something that will help with his image while this groping thing plays out.

Suddenly, Gabriel looks up. And right at me. It's startling. Like he knew I was looking at him. Like I'd somehow called to him. Our eyes lock. I immediately turn around to face the bar. Panic coasts through my veins and I'm not sure if it's because I'm worried he *will* recognize me or I'm worried that he won't. It was just one kiss. Five entire years ago.

Maybe he was too drunk to remember? Maybe I'm naive and remember it as more than it was. I mean... it was *just* a kiss. So why do I remember it like it was just yesterday?

3 / AXEL

New Year's Eve - Five years ago

I don't even know what I was thinking. I wasn't, clearly. I should have told him no, but Billy has always made that impossible. No isn't in his vocabulary. I shake my head as I navigate my way around the crowded interior of the yacht. There has got to be some code that's being broken with the amount of people on this thing. Yeah, it's enormous but seriously, I don't know how it's not sinking. There's got to be about five hundred people on this thing.

Five hundred minus one. I'm getting off. Just as soon as I find a way through the masses. As I weave and narrowly avoid getting a flute of champagne dumped on me by a drunk woman, I debate texting Billy again. He's the reason I'm here after all. He paid for my airline ticket and the five-star hotel room that I'm staying in.

He's the one who was invited to this fancy New Year's Eve party on this boat that costs more than I will make in a lifetime. At least it feels that way right now. My company is making progress but it's slow. And I'm scraping by. Billy's life is fancy yachts and five-star hotels because he's connected. It's part of his job to be, I guess. This boat has got to be owned by someone affiliated with racing, I assume, because it's Monaco and Billy is a Formula One driver. But honestly, I'm not sure. Everyone in Monaco is rich, it's like a birthright and you get a million euros with your birth certificate or something.

I slip past a waiter in a tux carrying an empty silver tray in one hand and an open bottle of gin in the other. The sight has me stopping for a heartbeat. Because the waiter is drop-dead fucking gorgeous and also, he's swigging the gin straight out of the bottle. Zero fucks given.

His eyes, which are a cobalt color, lock onto mine. The bottle is frozen to his lips. And those lips part in a mischievous smile as he swallows and then lifts the bottle in my direction. "Drink sir?"

I shake my head. If the staff is boozing it up, this party is officially out of control. The waiter is about two and a half feet from me. Two drunk girls wearing all the sequins stumble between us, giggling as they pass. The waiter holds up his empty silver tray to me after they're gone. "I would offer you an hors d'oeuvres but I'm fresh out."

"I see that." I nod. Man, he's way too hot to be a waiter, and I mentally smack myself for that thought. How fucking gross am I that I think hot people shouldn't be servers? Like their looks just make them eligible for more in life. My ex was right, I'm not a good person. That's what he told me when he said he needed to end things.

My phone buzzes in my pocket so I whip it out. Finally! Billy responded to my text telling him I was leaving.

> You are NOT. Stay. I will not let you wallow over that gaslighting arsehole. Stay. Get Fucked. Literally. I am.

And then another message.

I'll be done in a minute. Just gotta make her come. I'll find you.

I roll my eyes.

"Girlfriend trouble?" the waiter asks.

"Don't do girlfriends," I reply. "I'm here with someone but he's... busy."

"So maybe you should get busy too," the waiter replies. He sips from the bottle of gin again.

"Are you supposed to do that while working?" I am acting like a judgy schoolmarm or something. Typical me, my ex would say. Killjoy at heart. But seriously, something about this guy is off. And he looks familiar, but I've never been to Monaco before and he doesn't have an Australian or British accent, which are the two places I've spent the majority of my time in the last several years. London for school and Australia because it's home. His accent is faint. He speaks nearly perfect English but the struggle with the Hs and Rs makes me realize he's probably French. That's a common language in Monaco.

"Your brain is spinning. Why?" he asks me.

I shake my head. "Nothing. Never mind. Do you know the way off this ship?"

"Yep," he replies and then tilts his head like he's a puppy that heard a dog whistle. "But what just ran through your head? Because your expression just flickered with something sad. Like dark sad."

I twist up my features like I'm confused and hope he believes it. Then I rub the back of my neck. The collar on this shirt is too loose because it's one of Billy's, so I yanked off the tie and shoved it in my pocket a long time ago. "Not sad, just annoyed. I'm kind of over this scene and just want to go home."

"Home?" the waiter questions. "Aussie, right?"

I nod. "Yeah. But I'm staying at a hotel. Visiting a friend."

The waiter is still staring and the intensity of his gaze is a little much. But I like it. I wonder if he's gay. He's giving off the vibe, but I mean, I could just be projecting because I find him so attractive. "So can I like get a general direction from you? Left? Right? Where do I go?"

He takes another long sip from the open liquor bottle and then jerks his head, his shaggy light brown hair flipping back off his forehead. "Follow me."

He turns and walks and I follow. I don't know if I should, but... I mean he doesn't *seem* like a serial killer. Then again, my taste in men hasn't been great lately. Or, like, ever. My ex seemed nice, and kind, and not the type of guy who would dump me out of the blue, but he did. And then he gaslit me by making it feel like I deserved it for spending so much time at work. My company was months old and he knew it would consume me in the beginning. He even suggested he come work for me, so we could spend time together. He started being cold and cruel when I said I didn't think it was a good idea.

The waiter stops walking. He led me through the kitchen and now we're in a narrow passage that is unlike every other part of the yacht, empty. Probably because the sign on the door he pushed open said "crew-only". "You've got a dark, morose look on your incredibly attractive face. Are you sure this isn't the work of a girl?"

He's half smiling and I'm too stunned by the compliment to filter my response appropriately, so I blurt out, "A *guy*. He dumped me."

All the merriment and brashness slip from his features. "Well, then he's an idiot. You should know that."

I swallow and feel heat crawl up my neck to my cheeks. "He had some arguably decent points. I..."

All of a sudden his finger is pressed to my lips, so I can't move them. His skin is smooth and warm and soft. Not working class hands. Why does he look so familiar? He steps closer to me, his eyes searching mine. "Don't be that guy that explains away someone else's mistakes. You are too good-looking. He fucked up. You deserve better."

His finger drops from my lips. "You don't know me."

"You're right I don't," he replies. "But I still think you deserve better than you think you deserve. What does that say?"

"So... that exit?" I don't want to be psychoanalyzed by a waiter, no matter how hot he is, but what bugs me the most is he sounds like Billy. Billy has also told me I deserve better. It's been the only bone of contention in our friendship. But if my best friend thinks it, and this stranger thinks it, maybe it's true?

The waiter turns and starts walking again. The farther we walk down this corridor the quieter it gets. The thump of the DJ's music and the buzz of the chatter and laughter has dimmed significantly. He stops at the end of the hall, which parts to go left and right, and turns to me again. It's such an abrupt motion that I fail to stop before I bump into him. He uses his hand not holding the booze to grab my hip. His grip is firm and sends a spark of desire exploding like an errant firework in my abdomen. I'm glad he left that empty tray in the kitchen as we passed through.

"It's not even midnight yet," the waiter says, "but it's close. And if you leave now, you're going to ring in the New Year alone in the back of an Uber."

"It feels like a fitting end to a shitty year," I mutter. His hand hasn't moved from my hip. It should. I should step back so it does.

I don't move. I feel his fingers tighten a little and his expression looks earnest. He is truly a breath-taking man. He's clean-shaven, like me, and his tanned skin with an olive undertone is spectacular. His chin is dimpled. His lashes thick. His hair thicker. His lips just the right amount of plump and those eyes... Blue is my favorite color and eyes like his remind me why.

"I've had a shit year too, but here's the thing," he says and steps a little closer. "The new year isn't about the past, it's about the future. And I, for one, refuse to start next year as shitty as I end this one."

"People who look like you don't have shitty years," I blurt out. God, I'm such a loser. Who says things like that?

The waiter smiles, slowly. It's damn erotic to watch, which also makes me panic. I'm getting turned on by this stranger and I never do that. I'm Mr. Must Know Your Birthdate, Astrological Sign, and Criminal Record before I allow myself to think a man is cute.

"I like the way you blush," he tells me.

"You're working," I reply, which is nonsensical and not at all relevant.

"Am I?" he asks, which is just as nonsensical a response. But I don't have time to analyze it because he's offering me the gin bottle in his hand, and for some reason I don't understand, I'm accepting it.

I lift the bottle to my lips. My brain is screaming a list of my own rules getting broken here. I don't share drinks with anyone. I don't hit on strangers. I don't eye fuck strangers, and I'm pretty sure I'm doing that right now. I take a big gulp of the strong liquid and fight down a choke as I swallow.

He takes the bottle back and lets it drop to the floor. It lands with a hard thunk and tips over. I burst into action, dropping down and righting it before too much liquid can spill onto the gleaming hardwood floors. When I stand back up he's grinning. "You're one of the good ones, huh?"

"I... I mean I try."

"You succeed."

"That's a first," I retort and he blinks.

"Enough with the pity party," the waiter groans. His eyes are serious, I think. I mean I don't know him but he seems serious. "You know living well is the best revenge right? So live. *Well.* If you're not sure how, I can show you examples."

I bite my bottom lip like I always do when I'm stressed, which is most of the time. He reaches up and places the pad of his thumb flat against my lip, and with his fingers under my chin, he pulls my lip from its captivity between my teeth.

I step away from him. "Look, I don't know you. I don't do hook-ups or whatever. It's just... out of my comfort zone."

The roar of the crowd is pretty loud again but the thump of the DJ's music has disappeared. He is still holding my chin. "Who did you come with?"

"A friend."

"And where is that friend?"

Our eyes lock again. I feel another firework lighting up in my belly. "Fucking a girl somewhere on this boat."

He laughs. It's a light, carefree sound that is very appealing. And contagious. I feel my lips twitch into a smile. And then my phone buzzes. "So your friend knows how to live well, then. Even if you don't."

I start to walk away, moving past him, even though I'm more lost than ever now and have no idea where I'm going. When I feel his hand on my wrist I freeze. "Don't run away. It's almost midnight."

"So?'

"So I need someone to kiss."

I turn around. The movement pulls me a step away from him and he lets go of my wrist. Even though the proposition was bold, his expression is soft. But he starts to backtrack. "I mean, if you're not interested then no harm, no foul. Have a great night. But kissing someone at midnight, on New Year's, is good luck. And I could use some luck. And you could too."

"I... I..." I swallow. My heart starts beating harder and faster. "I don't kiss strangers."

"There's a lot of don'ts in your life."

He's not wrong. The year that's about to start suddenly plays in my brain like a movie preview. And all I see is work, sleep, weekends watching Netflix alone... that's it. Is that, as my mysterious waiter would say, living *well*? Suddenly the year seems like it would be a lot more interesting if I had this random encounter to look back on.

That roar of the crowd stops being a bunch of garbled noise and comes together in a countdown. "Ten. Nine. Eight."

I step into him. This stranger with a pretty face, a perfect smile, and no name.

"Seven. Six. Five."

He reaches up and brushes my cheek with his fingertips as his tongue slides across his bottom lip.

"Four. Three. Two."

"I'm Gabriel," he whispers.

"One."

I open my mouth to say my name but the boat erupts in cheers and whistles so loud I swear the floor and walls quiver. Then his mouth covers mine. He isn't shy. This is no sweet, cute peck. His tongue sweeps into my mouth, his hand wraps around the back of my neck, and his hips bump mine. I grab them to hold us together and do my best to keep up with the pace and emotion of this kiss. It's a tornado of lust and desire and nothing about it feels foreign, even though everything about him is.

This New Year's kiss tumbles into a New Year's make-out session. We're pawing each other as our mouths crush each other and our tongues battle for dominance. I can feel his dick hardening against my thigh at the same staggering rate as my own and then the swoosh of a door behind us has us jumping apart.

Someone yells his name. A needy, tipsy female voice. We both glance up and there's a pretty brunette in a halter dress. She calls out something in French and the only word I understand is "*papa*" which is French for dad.

"I have to go," he tells me.

"I thought that was my line." Oh. I'm witty when I'm aroused. That's new.

He grins. "Unlike if you leave, I'll be back. Carina over there just told me my dad is looking for me. He found out I've been parading around as a waiter and he doesn't think it's as funny as I do, apparently."

What? I blink. "Who is your dad?"

"My dad owns the boat," Gabriel grins at me like it's no big deal. "Louis Allard."

The party is being hosted by Allard Couture. The boat is owned by fashion mogul and self-made billionaire, Louis Allard. And I just had my tongue down his son's throat. Oh shit. This guy is officially, one hundred percent, out of my league. And I'm one thousand percent panicking.

He holds out his hand. "Come with me."

"Happy New Year," I croak out then rush down the hall to my left, pushing open the door and finding myself in a gaggle of people on a back deck. I start swimming through the crowd again and don't stop until I find the stairs that lead off the boat.

I never look back.

4 / GABRIEL

Yeah, I'm drunk and just sang in front of a group of strangers in a foreign country, but unless that guy trying to get into my pants slipped something in my drink, I am *not* high. Still, I swear I just hallucinated a guy I once kissed. Because why on earth would the tall, dark, and handsome Aussie from five years ago in Monaco be at a drag queen karaoke show in Montreal?

My feet move toward the hallucination in question. He's got his back to me now. Leaning on the bar, shoulders in, head bent like he's trying to hide. From me? I remember the way he grabbed at me, needy and rough, while I explored that perfect mouth of his. That's not something he should be hiding from.

He's holding up a hand talking to the bartender, ordering a drink... no wait. Another finger goes up. Two. He's with someone. Like I give a fuck. I hold up my own hand as my other one lands on his firm shoulder. "Make that three."

His muscles tense and I drop my hand as he turns around. Now I'm chest-to-chest with my former mystery kiss. He smiles, but it's tight and nervous. I smile back—all spice and heat.

"Hi," he croaks

"Hello. Again." He doesn't reply so I'm forced to add, "Remember me?"

"Yes," he replies swiftly before my ego can take a beating. "Of course."

I put my hands on either side of him on the bar, his head brushes past mine on the left, so close our cheeks scrape against each other. And then, with our bodies essentially pressed together, my voice is low and deep against his ear as I say, "This is crazy."

"You have no idea," is his response. He pulls back just enough so we're able to make eye contact again and then he says two blunt, bold words. "Listen, Gabriel."

"You can call me Gabe," I reply, which isn't a nickname I actually condone from just anyone. But him... yeah he can call me whatever he wants. "But you've never told me what I can call you."

"Axel." Finally after years of thinking about my mystery kiss, albeit not every second of the day but enough, I have a name. It feels like a victory for all of fourteen seconds until...

"Hey, Gabriel!" Billy James, a fellow F1 driver, tucks himself against the bar beside Axel.

The bartender drops the whiskeys on the bar, and Billy scoops one up. Axel grabs his but when I reach for mine he warns, "Do you really need another?"

I don't, but I grab it anyway. And then, without another word, I stalk off. Because I feel like a fish who was yanked out of the ocean and tossed onto the deck of a ship. Completely out of place and panicking. Billy James. He is *with* Billy James? Billy is my competition in more ways than one, it seems. And that kind of makes my stomach lurch. Not because I give a shit about both of us wanting the same man. I have no problem taking that on with anyone. But Billy is dating someone. A woman. His team principal. And I seriously doubt she knows about this. I wish I didn't. Not just because I'm gravely disappointed that my hot random hook-up bounced back into my life on this awkward wave, but also because I actually like Frankie. And Billy. Those two are on the very short list of people who don't go out of their way to remind me that I didn't earn my spot in F1. Frankie and Billy seem so in love. Like real love. The shit that is as elusive as a unicorn to me.

My thoughts are getting darker and darker, and so is my mood, which I would have thought impossible. Fuck, this world is full of shitheads. I swallow back the whiskey, which I hate, and decide to find that guy who wanted me. I need a distraction.

About an hour later, I'm still not distracted, even though I did find that guy and he's currently whispering some sexy bull-shit about what he wants to do to my cock, which should be getting me hard but isn't. And then I see Axel, out of the corner of my eye, walking to the bathrooms. I take a step away from my admirer. "Gotta go."

"What? Dude!"

I follow Axel.

5 / AXEL

I'M JUST FINISHING UP, washing my hands in front of the long line of black marble sinks, when Gabriel enters. I can tell by the way his eyes land on me immediately that he knew I was in here.

"Hey," I say.

He walks right over to me as I turn off the water and shake my wet hands. Before I can take half a step to the air dryer on the wall, he's blocked my path. His blue eyes are floating in booze, but his pupils aren't as big as saucers so it's likely he didn't take whatever his dance partner earlier was on. He pushes back his shoulders. He's a decent height, I'd say six feet even, but I've got a couple inches on him. Still, his presence is more than his height or slim build. He owns this space and is intimidating me. Maybe on purpose, maybe not, but it's happening.

"Look, I don't know what kind of guy you actually are, other than hot as fuck and an incredible kisser," he says bluntly and the pauses as his tongue darts out and wets his bottom lip. They're really nice lips and that tongue is pink and talented. He clears his throat, which makes my eyes move back up to his.

"But in case you *are* a decent guy with morals and shit, you should know that guy you've been with all night has a *girlfriend*. And I don't think she knows about this side of him. So yeah. FYI..."

He turns away abruptly and I reach out and grab his wrist without thinking. He turns back. "You rat people out all the time?"

It's a stupid conversation to have. I should just tell him who Billy and I are to each other, but this is really intriguing to me. Years ago, I thought he was a rich kid playboy. I was a plaything he had used for amusement and I didn't mind.

When I got tapped for this job, I figured maybe he *did* cross a line. Maybe. But clearly, he has boundaries and actively enforces right and wrong, in these types of situations, which makes me think the hesitation I felt the first time I heard the story of alleged inappropriate behavior was valid.

He frowns at my silence because my brain is running right now but my mouth isn't. "I don't lie. Not for anyone or to anyone. And I don't like compromising situations, if everyone involved doesn't know they're being compromised. I know you probably don't know this, since we never really met, just kissed. But I work with Billy and his girlfriend. I didn't think he was that type of guy, but I guess I'm shit at judgment."

"You're not shit at judgment," I reply. "Billy is my best friend. He's the reason I was on that boat years ago. And he's straight and ridiculously in love with Frankie."

Gabriel blinks, the shock bringing a hint of sobriety into his eyes. "So you're... visiting your best friend?"

"Something like that," I tell him. "I also have business in the area."

I realize in that moment, as a soft smile starts to bloom on his oh-so-handsome face, that I've still got my fingers wrapped around his wrist. I let go. He looks down at where my hand is now limp by my side and back up to my face. "Are you single?"

"Yeah."

"Still like kissing men?"

"I'm gay so it would suck if I didn't." Gabriel smiles at my smart-ass comment, which feels like a personal victory. I shouldn't be having flirty small talk with the guy I'm about to work for. *With*. Whatever.

"I'm bi, which is why I kissed you that night. And would kiss you again." Gabriel's smile gets deeper, and it suddenly feels like the AC got shut off in here. I watch his eyes rake over me slowly. His thoughts are dirty. I have no doubt about that and there is a part of me—bigger than it should be—that feels a thrill from that. "If you've known Billy for long, then you know who I am too."

"I figured out who you were before I even ran from that yacht. Google confirmed it."

He takes another few seconds, his eyes roaming my face with suspicion, before answering. "And you never used Billy to reach out?"

"No. I thought about it but..." I swallow. "I lived in Australia. You... were all over the place in F2. I didn't see how that could be anything."

"It could have been at least a weekend or two of fucking incredible sex," Gabriel replies, the smile parting his lips again. "You like to talk yourself out of things."

"You like to act without thinking," I reply. "Singing a song slamming the media when you're in the middle of a scandal is a stupid decision."

He blinks. "What are you referring to?"

"I work in public relations. I've been assigned, by your dad, to help handle this situation with your reputation. Rectify the damage done by the paternity suit and the current accusation by your dad's former assistant." He is just staring and blinking. I've blindsided him, I get it. "Let's talk about this more tomorrow. At the track. Sober and everything."

I walk by him and exit the bathroom, letting the crowd swallow me up as I weave my way to where I left Billy. He's moved from whiskey to beer and has a bottle poised near his mouth when he sees me approach. He grins. "Okay, there's a guy over in the corner who I think might be interested in you. He has been looking over here since you left. Like he's awaiting your return. What took you so long by the way?"

"I ran into Gabriel. Can we go?"

"What about the dude over there?" Billy does what he thinks is a subtle head tilt. It isn't. And I only look over to see if the guy noticed. He did. And he's getting off his stool.

"Not my type. Let's go. It's late and we both have to work tomorrow," I say flatly.

Billy sighs, takes one last sip of his beer, and puts the half-empty bottle on the bar.

"So what exactly is your type? I mean other than a total jerk who treats you badly and steals your company," Billy asks with a cheeky grin as we make our way toward the door.

I try to look pissy about that comment. But the truth is, I've missed Billy and his bluntness. We've kept in touch through the years but it's been a while since Billy and I have been in the same place at the same time since turning eighteen. Billy was on the race circuit. I got two degrees in England before heading back to Sydney to open my agency. The idea of spending regular time with Billy was a part of the reason I took this insane position. I mean, it wasn't the biggest part, but it factored in.

"You want my type? Okay. I like them thinner than that guy in the bar. And shorter. And with light eyes. A nice tan. In shape. And some intensity. That dude looks like he'd answer 'whatever you want' every time you ask him what he wants for dinner." When I'm done Billy's eyes are wide and blinking furiously. "What?"

"You just describe Allard."

"I did not."

"Yeah. You kind of did." Billy smirks. "He's tanned, a little shorter than you, in excellent shape, and his intensity is one of the reasons he needs a bunch of people to fix his reputation, including a fake boyfriend."

I turn to glare at my bestie walking beside me. I can see guys we pass checking him out. After all, Billy was born pretty. Also, thankfully for me, he was born without a judgmental bone in his body. I came out to him when we were sixteen. He's actually the first person I ever told. He was super quiet at first and my heart seized thinking I'd just lost my best friend. And then he said, "Cool. But look, I'm into girls so you can jerk off to thoughts of how hot I am, but that's it." To which I responded by calling him a fucking narcissist. And that was that. He never talks about my sexuality like it's any different than his own. Because it isn't.

"Ah... I'm right, aren't I? You think Gabriel is hot."

"He's not ugly," I mutter.

Billy laughs.

When we're in the hallway leading to the door. "I think Gabriel would have kissed me again tonight."

Billy's jaw drops, which is quite the feat. Nothing shocks him. He's usually the one doing the shocking. I feel a little surge of victory that I've finally done it to him after all these years. "You entertained the thought!"

"I didn't." The words leave my mouth so quickly they're coated in insincerity and Billy laughs so I relent. "Okay, I felt a desire to entertain the thought. I mean, he's hot. Undeniably. But I can't and you know that. Not for fun anyway. So I told him about the work thing."

Billy continues laughing as we step out of the club into the muggy Montreal night. For a place that's colder than a witch's tit eight months of the year, Canada sure as hell can do hot. Humid seems to be Montreal's middle name right now, in late August. "I wish I could've seen that exchange. I'm sure it was a car crash. The good kind, not the kind I'm usually in."

I roll my eyes as we turn left and stroll slowly down the sidewalk back toward our hotel, which is only four blocks away. He grins at me like I've just impressed him. "You are going to enjoy pretending to be Gabe's lover."

"It's a job," I reply.

Billy shakes his head, his blond hair glimmering gold in the moonlight. "Workplace romances are all the rage. Look at me and Frankie."

"Nope. Not for me."

"We'll see," Billy laughs.

I flip him the bird.

GETTING out of a Formula One car is a frustrating series of tasks. Undoing the six-point harness, removing the headrest, releasing and removing the steering wheel. It's a lot. We actually have to prove we can get out in five seconds or less, as a safety requirement, but today after practice I take my sweet time. Because I have to go deal with the media and then I have to go to the meeting with my dad, Damien, Henri, and Axel. Fucking Axel. I just don't want to deal with all of that, especially him. I can't believe my hot mystery kiss from half a decade ago is now the man in charge of cleaning up my dumpster fire of an image.

Aimee, the youngest, perkiest member of the Mayflower media team is waiting for me when I finally get out of the car and peel off my helmet, balaclava, and gloves. She hands me a bottle of water and levels me with her hundred-watt smile. "Good job out there. P5 is your best finish yet."

"It's a practice session, not a race. Not even qualifying," I mutter.

She nods. "Yup. But it's still something. Like it or not."

"Not," I grumble back at her. Her smile doesn't even falter. I think they assigned her to me because she doesn't let my black cloud of an attitude affect her at all.

She follows me as I walk toward the media. It's been drizzling today so they've been corralled under a tent. My fellow Mayflower driver, Sterling Samuels, is already halfway through the pack. A Lighthouse Racing driver, Cristian, is right in front of me. He smiles and stops his interview to shake my hand. "Great job out there, Allard."

"We'll see if I can do it again when it counts."

I feel Aimee's elbow in my back as Cristian goes back to his interview. "Stop scowling and next time at least give him a curt thanks."

Fucking hell. I hate getting lectured by this twenty-two-year-old ray of sunshine. But she isn't wrong. I growl out a sorry and step forward to talk to the first reporter. He also tells me I had a good session out there so I tell him "thank you" and glance at Aimee with a quick "happy now?" glare. She ignores me and continues to just stand there holding the digital recorder. Teams always record driver interviews so they can ensure they're never misquoted. And, in my case, so they can lecture me about how grumpy I get.

"I didn't expect that kind of placement from you today," the reporter says. "Rumor has it you were out pretty late last night."

Is he serious? I blink. "I didn't know that I wasn't allowed to leave the hotel room. Is that a rookie rule? Because Billy James was out last night. I saw him."

The reporter's eyes flare. He's like a dog who just caught a whiff of something stinky in the grass he's now dying to roll in. "Billy James was out with you?"

"Not with me. With his friend." Oh God, what have I started?

"At the *gay* bar you were at?"

"I said he was out. That's it. And honestly, I'm not here to talk about the social schedules of drivers, are you?"

Aimee visibly tenses beside me but doesn't say a word. She knows that's not her place but I get the feeling she would kick me if she could. The reporter clears his throat and changes topics. But that doesn't mean it's smooth sailing. "So, what changed out there? Why did you land in the top ten when you haven't been able to do that yet this year? How have you finally been able to put aside your off-track problems?"

"My off-track problems were never throwing off my driving," I reply, the defensiveness in my tone undeniable. "I haven't done any worse than a lot of other drivers in their rookie years. Look at Grady Lewis. We're doing about the same at the moment. I don't know what people were expecting. That I would finish on a podium every single race?"

"No people were not expecting that," the reporter clarifies. "But, you know, your seat could have gone to a great many other F2 drivers. So I guess, since you and your father and Mayflower Racing keep telling us it wasn't just the financing your father supplied that sealed your spot on the team, I guess maybe there is an expectation that you show us what did. You haven't finished over fifteenth so far this season. Haven't earned a single point for Mayflower."

This fucking asshole needs his microphone shoved up his ass. "Sterling Samuels finished in the top ten three times in his rookie season. All of those times were in the back end of the season."

"Okay. Sure. So you'll podium this season then? That's what you're promising?" he challenges.

I just made a bed I might not be able to lie in. I hate this guy. "I'm not promising anything. I'm just stating facts. You want to know anything about the actual practice session I just finished or should I just move on to a reporter who wants to do his job properly?"

Aimee inhales so sharply I hear it. The reporter lowers the microphone and levels me with a bit of a sneer. "You should probably move on. I'm sure you have other stuff to deal with after the media. Like that pesky lawsuit."

"Which one?' I quip and then bury his sneer in a cold smile of my own.

Without another word, I walk to the next reporter. Aimee glares at me as she shuffles along beside me. I guess I finally managed to drain the perkiness from her. Winning?

By the time I get to the meeting in the small conference room at the back of the second floor of the Mayflower Paddock, I'm in a worse mood than ever. My dad greets me with a proud smile, which makes me feel worse. "Congrats Gabriel!"

"It's just a practice session, Dad," I remind him as he walks past Axel, Damien, and Henri, who are sitting at the small conference table, to hug me. I try not to squirm. My dad is the best. He's always supported me and shown nothing but unconditional love to me my entire life. I'm an ass for being annoyed by his pride sometimes, like now. "But thanks."

He pulls back, still smiling proudly, and turns back to the people sitting at the table. "Okay. Let's get started. Introductions first. Gabriel, you know Damien and Henri but this is—"

I step around my dad and extend my hand. "Axel Walsh. Hello again."

Axel rises out of his seat slowly, carefully, like I'm a bear he just stumbled upon in the woods. "Hi. Again."

He slips his hand into mine and we shake. But I don't let go when it's done, or as my father exclaims, "You two have met?"

"Yes," I keep my eyes locked on Axel's deep brown ones. "I made out with him five years ago on your yacht."

I watch Axel's entire face turn a color that can best be described as volcanic tomato. It makes me want to laugh but I bite it back. Damien swears. Henri coughs up the coffee he's been sipping. My dad blinks. *"Pardon?"*

It sounds so regal and calm in French but what my dad is really saying is 'What the absolute fuck, Gabriel!' I can see it in the way his features start to harden and his eyes lose the light that had been bouncing in them.

Axel clears his throat and tugs his hand away from me. "I did *not* know who he was. And it was New Year's and I never... I mean, I didn't think it was relevant. It's not. It's not relevant."

Ouch.

My dad turns his attention to Axel. He seems to study him, and I kind of wish I knew what he was thinking. I realize that my addiction to shock value might cost Axel his job. I didn't think of that. Maybe I just shouldn't have opened my stupid mouth.

"Axel is right. It was absolutely nothing. Just a peck in a crowded room," I lie easily. "I just like being a drama queen Dad, you know that."

My father lets out a long, slow breath, as he thinks about that and decides whether or not to believe me. I meet his eye, holding his gaze with as much innocence as I can muster. Finally, he nods. "That's the kind of behavior that has us meeting today, Gabriel. Perhaps we need to start curbing it."

My dad. Tactful to a fault. I nod and drop down into a chair next to Damien. Axel slowly sinks into the chair next to Henri. He refuses to look at me and I guess I don't blame him. Dad walks back to his spot at the head of the table. He settles into his chair and places his elbows on the table, forearms flat against the wood, and fingers entwined. It's his 'down to business' pose, I always kid. It means he's been thinking about something, and he's come to a decision.

"So, if you two are already acquainted then this will be easier than I thought," he says. And then he smiles. Something about it makes my blood chill, which never happens. I trust my dad's judgment on basically everything. But my body is reacting in a very bad way right now.

"Feels like a sign that this is not just the easiest solution but the right one," Damien says and looks at Axel for confirmation.

Axel kind of shrugs and nods at the same time.

"What plan is this?" I ask, and now the hair on the back of my neck is standing at attention too.

"We're settling you down," my father announces. He is fluently bilingual, but sometimes he gets flustered and doesn't exactly say what he means in English.

"*Dit-moi en Francais,*" I command, figuring he might make more sense in our mother tongue.

"*Tu vas sortir avec Axel.*" I stare at him, cluelessly. "*Il sera ton petit copain. Jusqu'à ce que ça se calme.*"

I keep staring at my dad as the words swirl around in my brain, not making any sense. "You hired me a boyfriend?"

"I hired you a public relations consultant who is going to play the role of your boyfriend," he clarifies.

I turn my head slowly until my blue eyes meet Axel's brown ones. He is no longer volcanic tomato. Now he's more of a Casper white. Petrified porcelain. "You've whored yourself out for this?"

"I took the assignment, yeah," Axel replies. "It's a normal tactic. Celebrities do it all the time, and I... fit the bill for this. For you."

"Because you're hot and a good kisser?"

And now he's volcanic tomato again.

"I'm sure the kissing thing will help," my dad interjects.

Oh my fucking God. "This is insane. No. This is not going to happen."

"Listen, kid," Damien says because he always calls me kid even though he's maybe fifty, not some old grandpa. He's been on my father's legal team since he was thirty and I hadn't grown hair on my balls yet so whatever. "I know you're a free sexual spirit. I admire it, actually. But let's be honest, most of this bullshit stems from that. The woman accused you of fathering that kid because you *did* fuck her. And the assistant with the chip on her shoulder, she accused you because she thought it was believable."

"Also she knows my father will fix my problems. Everyone knows that," I snap and push back my chair.

"*Gabriel, non. S'il te plait.*" His words are polite, but his tone has an edge.

I don't stand, but I don't pull my chair back in either. "I don't want a fake boyfriend. Even one who can kiss. You want me to date someone, I'll find someone who will do it willingly."

"And sign an NDA? And accept payment? And not make a bigger mess later because they get their feelings involved and you don't?" Henri asks. "Hate to break it to you but this is the sensible option."

I open my mouth but no words come out. I glance at Axel who is watching me intently, but with no expression I can decipher. I suddenly feel like a child at the adult table of a holiday party. Like I don't belong and everyone is just kind of placating me. Even Axel.

"This is the best idea we have?" I demand.

"Yeah," Henri admits, and he's not even the least bit sheepish about it. "This is the optics part. Damien is working on the legal part. There's a lot more tactical stuff with that."

"I've subpoenaed the shit out of everyone on that plane, and the company that owns it, and the pilots," he announces proudly.

"And I'll pay her if all else fails."

"And I will quit racing if you do," I remind him. We've had this conversation before. "I am not going to walk around with even the slightest doubt in people's minds that I touch people without their permission. I don't. I didn't. I am *not* paying her a fucking cent."

My father rolls his eyes, sick of what he considers 'my antics'. "Gabriel, let's just cross that bridge when we come to it."

"*If* you come to it," Axel interjects. "In the meantime, let's discuss this arrangement. I think if you understand why it has to happen, and what results we hope to get, you'll be more comfortable."

I stand up. "I'll be more comfortable when I'm back at the hotel, showered, and fed. I'm sweaty, exhausted, and done with this conversation."

I walk out of the room, but over my shoulder I add, "Axel, feel free to swing by my room in a couple hours to discuss this further."

I don't bother to wait to hear Axel's objection.

WITH EVERY FLOOR the elevator climbs, the more antsy I get about it. That meeting went so badly that it was almost laughable. Not to mention that Damien pulled me aside afterward and reamed me out for not mentioning that I had been involved with Gabriel. I explained "involved" was a stretch, but he didn't care. Henri said I made him look bad to Louis because he was the one who suggested me. Louis didn't seem to care, in fact, if anything, he saw it as a bonus. He thought we would be more at ease with each other. Ease is not what I'm feeling as the elevator doors open on Gabriel's floor and I make my way to his suite.

I rap my knuckles on the door and it flies open a second later. He's standing there in the hotel robe. White, thick, but loosely tied so half his sculpted bare chest is on display. "Spoiler alert: bathrobes for meetings are inappropriate."

He rolls his eyes. "Well, I was naked when you knocked so you're lucky I put on anything. I'll change. Just come in."

I step inside and he turns and marches through the suite and into the bedroom. In front of me is a huge living room, with a glitzy mirrored bar and coffee station and a pink velvet couch by the window that overlooks the Leonard Cohen mural on Crescent Street below. In front of the couch is a room service tray covered in food. I have no idea what any of it is though, because the silver dome lids are covering everything. But the entire room is filled with delicious, savory scents.

I realize I'm ravenous.

"I ordered a few things because I have no idea what you eat," Gabriel calls out from the bedroom. The door is open but I can't see him, which is a good thing. "There's a grilled halloumi salad which is sent from heaven if you're a vegetarian and there's a poached salmon dish with a lobster butter sauce and good old American burgers and fries."

He emerges from the bedroom. His hair is damp, which I must have missed before. Too busy staring at his bare chest, I guess. Now he's changed into a pair of deep blue pajama bottoms made out of some kind of soft-looking fabric that clings to him like a needy kitten. But nothing else. I frown at him. He pushes back his bare shoulders defiantly. "Look, I spend hours in layers of fire retardant clothing sweating my ass off. I hate piling on more layers at home. So just deal with it. Also, I've had meetings with a lot of people looking like this so you're not special, I promise."

Ouch. Okay then. I move toward the couch and sit as far as possible on one end so he has lots of space. It's not a huge couch and it's curved, almost kidney-shaped. He watches me shift and wiggle with an amused smirk, but he doesn't say anything. He sits down square in the middle of the couch and starts pulling lids off the food. "I wasn't sure if you'd show up or quit."

"I don't scare easily. I just look like I do," I reply.

He slides a plate with the burger and fries on it to my end of the table. "How about we half everything? That way no one's taste buds get FOMO."

I have to bite the inside of my cheek to keep from laughing. I don't know why I don't want him to think I find him charming.

He hands me a knife and I cut the burger in half while he dresses the salad.

The next several minutes are spent in silence as we eat. We both drink ice water with lime and raspberries floating in it. It isn't until he leans over and steals a fry that we start talking.

"Why did you take this job?" he asks after he swallows down the fry.

"Because I needed a job," I reply and sip my water. "Now let's talk about how we're going to make this work. I'll go first. You stop trying to humiliate me in front of your father. Or anyone."

He laughs, leaning back into the sofa, stretching his long defined arms across the back like he hasn't a care in the world. "How does one go from creating and running the most successful public relations firm in Australia to agreeing to be a boyfriend to a race car driver in a marketing ploy?"

I promised myself I would stay calm and focused and not let Gabriel ruffle me, but that did it. My eyes flare and my jaw tenses so hard I swear I might have cracked a molar. His inky eyes absorb my reaction and a small, almost sympathetic smile plays on his lips. "I figured now that I know your name, I get to Google you too."

"Fair enough, I guess," I mutter and exhale long and slow, forcing myself to unclamp my jaw too. He's waiting intently for an answer. "I had a bad break-up and needed to try something new."

I don't elaborate that I needed to try something new because my ex took my biggest accounts with him when he walked out the door on me, and the company I'd allowed him to work for without a non-compete clause. Because I was in love and trusted him. I decide to change the subject, or at least veer us back to work. Because that's what I'm here for, not to share my deepest humiliations.

"If you want a different person to be your fake boyfriend, that can be arranged," I tell him as I lean forward, putting my elbows on my knees. "But your father will want to vet them as thoroughly as he vetted me which will cost us time. We were hoping to get this started tomorrow."

"How the hell is this going to fix anything?" Gabriel stands up and walks to the bar. He pulls open the door of the small fridge and peers at the contents.

"Optics matter. You've been this careless playboy your entire life," Axel replies. "Do you know that after we met, when I Googled you, every candid picture that came up was you doing something intimate with someone. You kissing a girl on a yacht in Croatia. You with your hand on some girl's ass at a bar in Spain. You in the States grabbing some guy by the hair."

"That was Austin," Gabriel explains as he pulls two bottles of beer from the fridge. "I know the headline on that tabloid was something about me getting aggressive but he likes things rough. He got off on me yanking on his hair or slapping his ass. He likes biting too but I refused."

"He had a bite mark on his shoulder a few days later when he was photographed at a farmer's market," I remind him, because yeah, I deep-dived Gabriel long before I had to.

"Wasn't me. Get a dentist to analyze the bite mark." Gabriel walks a little closer and offers me one of the beers but I shake my head so he puts it down on the coffee table and twists the cap off his. "We weren't exclusive. I don't do exclusive so I don't know where that bite came from but it wasn't me."

"Well, it looked like it was you and you do exclusive now," I reply and he lifts an eyebrow. "I mean, you'll pretend you do. This should only have to go on until the case is dropped. Damien is really confident that we can do that before the end of the season."

Gabriel huffs out a breath that says he's not so sure and then turns and walks to the window. He stares out at the twinkling lights of the Canadian city. The Leonard Cohen mural has soft white lights illuminating it from the bottom, giving the soulful singer a melancholy glow. I feel like Gabriel has that same aura right now.

"I said it doesn't have to be me."

I stand up and walk the short distance to stand kind of behind him. He shakes his head without looking at me. "The fact that it's you is the only part of this plan I like."

Oof. I feel that deep in my chest. His words are like a warm blanket. But they can't be. I'm the worst with men. Why is it the slightest compliment and I'm batting my eyelashes as my heart flutters wildly? "Thanks. I think."

He raises an eyebrow again but I ignore it and continue my pitch. Louis warned me his son would need coaxing. "Look, we hang out a little tomorrow, in the paddock and around the track when you aren't busy. Then repeat it at the next few races. Then we may spend a couple days on a beach or boat somewhere if Damien hasn't rectified this by the time break comes around. Separate rooms, just some public shots."

"Well, where is the fun in that?"

I shouldn't smile but I do. Because he's smiling and it's bloody contagious. I feel my cheeks start to heat too. "This is work."

"If I had a fragile ego, you would have shattered it by now," Gabriel announces, and then he brushes by me, his arm rubbing mine and discharging that unexpected firework of desire in my gut like it did that New Year's. "Lucky for you, I don't. And I think you're a liar."

I bristle. "Excuse me."

"This isn't just work for you," Gabriel says and puts the beer bottle to his mouth. I watch him swig back a mouthful with much more interest than normal, which proves his point.

"You could have said no to this assignment. You seem like the type of guy who would. All morals and character and boundaries."

If only...

"Look, I admit the fact that it was you made this easier, but I also get to be around Billy. And it's a position I've put other people in when I ran a PR company, so maybe it also felt like it was my turn to be in this position." I give him that. I don't want to tell him that the reward for this is also what drove me. I get promoted, immediately, when this is over and my career and my ego, which is much more fragile than Gabriel's, need that. "But I'm not looking for a relationship right now. I just came out of one that... well let's just say some rollercoasters have fewer ups and downs than we did. And I'm looking for smooth sailing right now."

"Okay."

I move my eyes from the piece of carpet I was focused on while I gave that little speech and meet his eye. He's watching me curiously. "Okay, what?"

"Okay fine. I'll go along with this stupid plan and pretend we're dating," Gabriel announces. "But I need to get on a call in five minutes with my strategists so let's just pick this up in the morning. We'll share a car to the track and you can hold my hand and make heart eyes at me. Sound good?"

I think he's kidding about the hand-holding. Maybe? I don't ask. I simply make my way to the door. I got what I came for—buy-in to this PR smoke show. I open the door and turn. He's right there, a foot behind me.

"So I'll see you tomorrow."

He nods, leaning on the door, keeping it open as I step into the hall. I should be walking away, but I'm stuck staring at him like his stare has pinned my feet to the floor. "If you're looking for a good night kiss, boyfriend, I don't do fake ones. Only real ones. And I don't want to kiss you good night. I want to kiss you good morning."

My face heats and my legs finally start working again thanks to fear. The fear that his flattering words will go straight to my head... or my dick.

I hear him chuckling to himself as I walk away. I hate that he's so amused by my awkwardness. I hate that I'm awkward. I have incredible business smarts. I built a successful company, made brands millions, saved the reputations of celebrities, but yet when it comes to men... emotionally I'm still a clueless teenager. And I let my inability to deal with a relationship cost me my business. It's humiliating and I am not going to let it happen again. So I keep walking away from Gabriel, never turning back.

It's a cloudless, clear day. Hot and humid. Not the best conditions for me. I'm a driver who excels in rain and damp conditions, like during yesterday's practice. I don't know if I'll be able to qualify as high as I placed in practice with these conditions. It's not likely. Luckily no one seems to care what I do.

I walk over to my race car and pause to adjust my helmet before climbing in. I've got what I lovingly refer to as the Z-Squad working with me. Sterling Samuels has our top engineers, mechanics, hell even our best PR person by his side every day. I've got the rest. I mean, to be fair, you don't get to work for a Formula One team unless you're better than most at your given profession, but still, there's a hierarchy and it's clear I am not the crown prince. I'm the court jester who paid for his title so no one takes me seriously.

I can see Axel in the corner of the garage, he's got his phone in his hands but he's not looking at it. He's eyeballing me. I wink at him and he gives me a quick, tight smile before he actually does move his eyes to his phone. See, that's never going to work. The tightness on his features when we look at each other.

I climb into the car, slip into place, and get strapped in. Then I flip down my visor just as the stupid documentary crew for the reality show that follows the drivers turns its lens toward me. I hate them, mostly because they rarely give me any coverage. They've sat my father down for more interviews than they have me. It's humiliating, but I signed on for it when I let my dad pay for this seat. I stupidly thought I would prove my worth. I haven't placed yet this season. But, I mean, that's actually not unusual for a rookie. It's just I have to be more than usual. Average. Normal.

I get the all-clear to drive out of the garage and I go down the pit lane with laser focus. As my foot presses harder and harder on the gas, exiting the pit lane, I push thoughts of anything but the track out of my head. I let my heart and soul fall into 'the zone' as I call it.

Qualifying can be a brutal process in the best of conditions. The qualifying session lasts one hour and is divided into three knock-out stages—Q1, Q2, Q3, with small intervals in between. The five lowest times get dropped at the end of each round, giving them their place on the grid. I surprised everyone, even myself, by making it to Q1. That means I'm starting in the top ten no matter what happened this last round.

I feel like I'm in good form as I move around the track for Q1. Despite the humid air and the dry track I hit every turn just right but struggle in the chicane. My heart leaps into my throat as I slide a little coming out of it, over the line. If all four tires cross, my lap time won't count. I can't tell if they do from my position, so I focus on getting to the finish line so I will have enough time to go again. But then our race engineer, Pablo Paloma's voice fills my ear through the radio. "Yellow flag. Yellow flag. A Mirabella car is in the wall by the turn eight."

That means debris litters the track. We have to lower our speed. And it also means I probably won't have time for another lap to improve my time and I'm kind of fucked if my previous lap gets thrown out. Still, I have bigger concerns.

"Who was it?" I ask through the radio.

"Umm... Castera."

"Is she okay?" I shoot back immediately. Lucia Castera was in a huge fiery crash in F2. I was out there, with her, when it happened. I could see the ball of fire engulf her and her car as I drove past the crash. It was the most horrifying thing I've ever seen. She miraculously made it out with only a small burn to her hand.

"Fine. She's already out of the car. Focus on you, Gabriel."

"I can multitask, thanks," I snap.

Yeah, that's not going to win me favors but fuck him if he thinks I'm not going to worry about another driver. It isn't long until we get the green light again, but I don't make it to the start line before time runs out.

I swear a blue streak until Pablo interrupts me. "No need for the potty mouth, Gabriel. You finished ninth."

Ninth!

"Really?"

"Yes. Congrats."

"Thanks." I keep my tone chill but inside I'm screaming with excitement. It's my first time qualifying in the top ten. If I manage to keep my spot through the race tomorrow, which might happen, then I'll earn my first points in F1. This is a big deal.

When I get the car into the garage, I'm greeted by only four people. A couple mechanics, my dad, and Axel. Everyone else is watching Sterling do interviews because he qualified third. I wish it didn't deflate my emotions, but it does. And it batters my ego just a little bit. I'm like a helium balloon with a slow leak.

My dad is beaming at me. "Amazing job, Gabriel. I know the conditions weren't your favorite."

"If I could have squeaked in another lap I could have gotten higher, I know it," I say softly as he leans in for a hug after I pull off my helmet and fireproof balaclava.

Axel is standing beside my dad and he lifts his hands, like he might reach for his own hug but then shoves them in his pockets. Because *that's* not awkward. His weirdness is not just amusing to me, but appealing. He gives me a pained smile. "Great finish!"

I laugh under my breath and step right into him. I cup the back of his head and pull his face to mine, planting a firm but chaste kiss on his stunned mouth. "Thanks, babe!"

My dad's smile slips, and he leans closer. "Easy, now."

I sling an arm around Axel's shoulders. "Sorry if you thought I was going to go about this like a tween crush."

Axel's pale skin is red and his eyes are a little wide but he nods. "He's right, Mr. Allard. Your son isn't exactly known for being subtle. We have to sell this."

"Then drop the Mr. Allard and call me Louis in public," Dad suggests with a small nod.

I give Axel's shoulder a squeeze before letting go and walking over to Aimee who is waiting patiently to walk with me to the media gallery. "See you back in my dressing room?"

I wink and Axel gets redder but nods.

Maybe this is going to be fun after all. I mean, I kind of love making him uncomfortable.

THIS IS GOING to be much harder than I thought. And I thought it was going to be a struggle of epic proportions. I stand in the corner of the room watching Louis pace and Damien sit with his arms folded sternly across his chest. Zack stands with his hands on his wide hips in the open door to the conference room.

It's been a week. We've moved on from Montreal, where Gabriel finished eleventh. Not in the points, which are only given to the top ten, but the closest he's come. Now we're in Miami. The Mayflower team is in their element, being American-based. I am in hell. It's hot, the track is an over-the-top spectacle, and Gabriel is still not doing himself any favors. He's playing along with me in public—walking close to me, rubbing my back, whispering in my ear, kissing my cheek—but he is being a complete arsehole with the media.

"You're going to have to handle this too, obviously," Bob Johnson announces and Louis looks up at him with a scowl that can only be described as withering.

In that glare, I can see the cut-throat businessman gleaming in his hazel eyes. The guy who built a fashion empire from scratch and raised a son alone and would burn the world to the ground to save either. "I thought you had staff for this? Perhaps if you assigned him a public relations person that wasn't in diapers we wouldn't be having this conversation."

Bob frowns, creating large rolls on his forehead. "Even if we assigned him someone else, he likely wouldn't listen to them either so I'm not wasting my time or resources."

Bob turns and leaves. Louis hisses out something in French which I'm sure is vulgar but I don't understand it. Damien does though, being bilingual, and his eyes flare but he doesn't say anything. We all just heard about the last few press interviews Gabriel had given this weekend. He's flippant and downright rude with a lot of the reporters because a lot of them are asking questions about this lawsuit and not the race he just finished.

He qualified tenth, but finished the race twelfth today, by no fault of his own. His mechanics fucked up a tire change on lap forty-four and then he had an unsafe release. That means he entered the pit lane, to head back onto the track when another driver was already in it, and he could have caused a crash. That's the fault of the team because they're the ones who tell the driver when they can enter. He got a five-second time penalty for that. If he hadn't had the penalty he would have finished ninth. Points. And so yeah, he was pissed and it was a big deal and I was worried the media would push all his buttons about it. But instead, they asked him questions about the lawsuit because the woman making the accusation did an interview with Figaro, a French paper. And Gabriel exploded, actually telling one reporter to *"Fermez votre gueule"* which is the rudest French way to say 'shut your mouth'.

Damien turns to me. "Why aren't they talking about you? That's the whole point of this charade. If they're asking about you, they aren't asking about her."

"They should be asking about his driving," I remind

everyone but no one seems to care about that. "He's doing better every race."

"You need to handle this, Axel," Louis informs me sharply so I know this isn't up for debate. "Talk to him. He clearly isn't listening to me anymore."

Louis actually looks hurt when he says that. I watch him pace in the small space, his hands running absently over the front of his Allard Couture sport coat. He looks his age for the first time since I met him. He's sixty if his Wikipedia profile is to be believed, but he barely looks fifty, until now. Yes, his hair is salt-n-pepper but the salt part is a stunning, bright silver color. And unless he's upset, like now, his skin is smooth, wrinkle-free except for the crow's feet when he flashes a smile equally as mischievous as his son's.

I feel for him. I know he's just trying to make his only child's life easier and his dream a reality. I clear my throat and nod. "I'll handle it."

I step out of the room without another word and cross the small corridor to Gabriel's dressing room. The only person in there is his trainer, Enzo, who is packing up. "He left. Said he would stretch in the hotel sauna before the flight to Vegas tonight."

I nod and move to the stairs to head down and find my car and driver so I can catch Gabriel before his steam. But I only make it to the bottom of the stairs before Damien calls my name. He comes marching down after me, his expression stern. "Listen, you have to do more."

"I'm on my way to Gabriel right now to make sure future interviews go more smoothly," I tell him and swallow down the frustration building in me. I've decided, over the last ten days, I don't like Damien much. He's been with Allard Couture for over a decade and clearly Louis has no issue with him. But I find him abrasive and smug and his solution to all of the Allard business problems seems to be to spend money to make someone else handle it. He, himself, doesn't seem to handle much of anything except the perks of the job—free travel, hotels, and dinners.

"Not that shit. I mean, yeah, fix that, but you have to get your little relationship out there in a big way. Fast," Damien warns, and his wide mouth presses into a firm line as he glares at me.

"We are pretty damn public," I remind him. "It's not my fault the cameras don't catch it."

"Then fuck him on his damn car if that's what it takes," Damien argues, his head tipped toward me and his voice low so that any Mayflower staff wandering by doesn't overhear.

"PDA is fine but I'm not whoring myself out," I snap.

He rolls his eyes like I'm an overdramatic teenager. "You need to figure out a way to sell it better, without compromising your precious morals, because this isn't working fast enough. And if it isn't working, I will tell Louis to cut his losses."

"I'll make it work," I promise, forcing my voice to stay calm and assured instead of bitchy and bitter, which is really how I want to sound.

Damien makes it worse by adding, "It's Allard's reputation on the line here. Yours is already in the shitter. This is your chance at redemption and you're only getting one. You want to leapfrog everyone into the director position, I need to see this working. Fast. Or else we can hire an external firm. Like Fast Fix."

Fast Fix. Wow, Damien went from verbally sparing to punching below the belt with that one. Fast Fix is the name of the public relations and brand management company my ex started last year when he walked out on me.

I inhale and it's shaky, but I refuse to acknowledge that threat. I really fucking hate Damien and that's just more reason to get this job done right. So I can leapfrog, as he put it, and get the hell away from him, and get my life back on track.

I walk out the paddock doors, promising through gritted teeth that I will get the job done.

Now to find Gabriel and convince him, because that's who this hinges on.

Aᴍ I surprised when the sauna door opens and Axel steps inside the small, dark, humid room? Nope. I figured they'd send him. Actually—correction—I knew they would send *someone*. I hoped it would be *him*.

He stands in front of me, barefoot but fully dressed, which is so absurd I smile. "You're probably violating some kind of hotel policy. I don't think they allow you in here with all those clothes on. It might even be a safety hazard."

"Oh well," Axel replies and folds his arms across that broad, sculpted chest of his. I don't know how often he works out, but it must be a lot because the man is all lean, sculpted muscle. "You need to stop throwing tantrums with shitty reporters. You're feeding into their image of you as a selfish, spoiled rich kid who gets away with murder. And assault."

Wow. He came out swinging. All-business Axel is hot, by the way. Five stars. Highly recommend. Almost makes me want to be a bigger brat next presser. Except I know if I don't listen to him, my father might step in, so I guess I should listen. Still, right now there's no harm in playing. I lean back, spreading my arms across the sleek wood bench. "So, how do you propose I handle it when all they want to ask about is the fact they think I'm a predator instead of the fact that I am starting in the points regularly now?"

Things did not go well with the media after qualifying. The same reporter who came at me the other day, who I found out is called Nico Hilliard, came at me again. And I snapped, again. Axel stares hard as if waiting for me to answer my own question because it's that obvious. Then he rolls his dark, delicious eyes and tells me the answer he wants to hear. "If you have questions that pertain to off-track events please consult my lawyer. But I can tell you anything you need to know about the race. The qualifying session. The practice. Insert whatever stupid part of F1 events here."

His voice was amusingly bright during that little speech, which makes the scowl on his face all the more jarring. Axel gives good annoyed parent face. I nod slowly, my eyes watching the perspiration bead on his forehead. "I'm not sure I get it. Repeat that, just so it sinks in, please?"

The glare ratchets up. I have to bite the inside of my cheek to keep from smiling. I lift an arm off the bench and motion toward him. "Maybe you should take your clothes off. Before you melt into a puddle."

"I'm not staying."

"You should. Saunas are great for detoxifying," I explain and let my smile finally play on my lips. "And you definitely seem to need to let the toxins out."

He hisses out a 'fucking hell' and then his gaze gets less annoyed and more...serious. "I thought you gave a shit about this career. Am I wrong?"

"You are not wrong," I reply without hesitation. "But I'm destined for failure. I've accepted it."

That hits him like a slap. He blinks and all emotion slips off his face for a second. He wipes his brow. "You're a talented driver. You work your ass off. You killed it in F2. Points every race your last season, finishing second overall. If you'd waited it out a season longer you'd have been offered a seat. You didn't need to buy your way in. But regardless, you still have the potential to really make a name for yourself in F1 the same way you did in those lower levels."

He's watched my career? Now it's my turn to be stunned. I lean forward, putting my elbows on my knees, which are spread. I have a feeling the towel around my waist is precariously close to opening and I'm not wearing anything under it. "But the fact is everyone knows my dad bought my seat at Mayflower. It was always going to be an uphill battle to gain credibility, but I thought I could do it. One year at Mayflower, and then someone else would want me based on *me*. On my performance, not my parentage. But now... with the paternity debacle and this assault charge, no one will want to touch me, even if I win the championship, which spoiler alert, I'm not going to. It's a lost cause."

Axel shakes his head before I even finish speaking. "That's bullshit and you know it or else you would have quit by now."

A bead of sweat slips from the dark hair at his temple and slides down his face. I stand up. "Have you met my father? He wouldn't let me quit because it would mean he failed. I'm his only child. One he went through a lot to have, so my failures and successes are his. He's invested. I may see the inevitable end to this career but I have to let it come naturally. He won't see it any other way."

Axel sighs. I'm directly in front of him now, standing so close he's almost blurry. "Take off your clothes. This is silly."

"I'm not staying."

"But yet, you're not going," I reply and tug the tie on my towel. It breaks free of my hips and I take the end and lift it to wipe the trail of sweat off his temple.

He doesn't flinch. Because his head is tipped slightly down, his jaw hanging open, and his eyes are glued to my exposed semi-hard cock. When his temple is dry and the towel hangs loosely in my hand by my side, he raises his head so our eyes meet. His gaze is dark and stormy and the desire in that darkness is undeniable. My cock swells a little bit more. "I'm not your whore. I'm not paid to—"

"I'm not asking you to do anything," I interrupt and start to tie the towel back around my waist. "But let's be clear, if you did do something, it wouldn't be part of this stupid job. It would be because the personal business we have is unfinished. I should have fucked you senseless on that yacht and you know it."

"I know that... this is a different time and a different situation." Axel swallows so hard his Adam's apple looks like it's trying to break the smooth skin of his neck.

"You still attracted to me?"

"Yes."

"And I still want you," I reply and step closer to him again. This time I keep my towel on but reach for the hem of his shirt, my fingers skirting it gently. "I think you can see that."

"Damien is mad. He thinks we aren't selling this hard and fast enough," Axel blurts out, and it's clear he doesn't realize the double entendre in his words until I smile. Then he turns red and I let out a breathy laugh. "God, you don't stop do you?"

"Do you want me to stop?" I ask the question that's been plaguing me since he walked back into my life. The one I'm not sure I want the answer to. "Because I know I'm coming on kind of strong, but I will stop. If you really don't remember how fucking hot that kiss was and don't feel any of that chemistry we had, then I will back off and this will actually be a boring business arrangement and nothing more. Unlike what that woman says about me, I *do* take no for an answer."

I finally shut up and wait, impatiently, for Axel to tell me something—good or bad. He inhales slowly and exhales even slower. "I feel it. Still. Again. I feel the chemistry. It's why I took the job. Because I knew I'd feel it and it would be easy to sell us."

Fuck, yes! I try not to look as relieved as I feel. Gotta be cool. Calm. Collected. Axel scares easily. But I dare to step even closer to him, with a firmer hold on the hem of his shirt. "You should take this off. You're melting."

I start to pull his shirt up. He actually lets me get it all the way over his head. And then he really blows my mind because he reaches for the knot on my towel.

The feel of his fingers curling around the Terry cloth sends heat ricocheting down my spine. White, hot desire. I grab the back of his neck but hesitate. I need to be sure he wants this. He yanks the towel before I can even say a word, pulling our bodies together until our lips connect. I could whimper with relief. Instead, I open my mouth and find his eager tongue with my own.

The kiss is New Year's Eve all over again. Hot and needy and wild. I'm still the more dominant one, but Axel is submissive in all the best ways. He melts into me, and if I slow the pace of our kisses, he groans and holds tighter to my towel, and flexes his hips into me. Axel is as hard as I am.

And I'm about to do something about it when the door to the sauna opens.

I'm kissing him. Gabriel's lips are on mine, his tongue is in my mouth, and his teeth are nipping my bottom lip, just like he did five years ago when I thought he was a horny inappropriate waiter. And I feel... joy. It's the most odd but amazing sensation. Kissing him with abandon makes me feel young, free and hopeful. Because I haven't done anything with abandon since the last time I kissed him.

And just like I always feared, I'm going to pay for it.

The door opens and hits me square in the back, pushing me roughly into Gabriel who stumbles backward. We're both thrown into reality with the gust of cool air that accompanies the intrusion.

"Oh. Sorry!"

I grab my shirt off the floor brush by the person who entered and head out of the sauna without looking up. Gabriel doesn't follow, which is for the best. I need to have a stern, judgmental conversation with myself before I can face him. I just made out with my client... well, my client's son who is my project. In a public space. While on the clock. I mean, yes my job is to pretend to be his boyfriend, but that crossed lines. I would have dropped to my knees and sucked him off if we hadn't been interrupted. My lust for him has knocked me senseless.

Gabriel is a live wire. He runs hot all the time in his car, in his social life, which has proven to be a problem, and with his emotions. It's the polar opposite of me, of my instincts, and it's a total, utter turn-on. It's also a fucking nightmare. As if I needed salt poured into my emotional wound, as soon as I open the door to my hotel room—shivering because the sweat that coats my body is now cold—my cell starts buzzing. I yank off my shirt, which is damp and gross, and drop it on the floor as I pull my phone from my back pocket with shaking hands. My sister's name illuminates the screen. Great. I inhale and answer. "Cordy."

"Hey pumpkin," she says in a light airy voice. "And it's Delia now, remember? When I'm calling as a realtor, it's Delia."

My sister's name is Cordelia however we've always called her Cordy. She runs the hottest up-and-coming luxury real estate company in Australia and has now decided that Delia, not Cordy or Cordelia, is the right name for a person who owns that sort of business.

"I have good news and I have good news!" she announces. "What do you want first?"

Normally I find my sister's upbeat, quirky personality endearing but I'm so not in the head space for this. "Can we cut to the chase, Cor... Delia. I have to catch a plane to Vegas."

"They don't fly you private?" she counters, and a gasp leaves her mouth which is ridiculous.

"They do."

"So the plane will wait for you, hot shot," Cordy replies. "Anyway, first good news. I have a full-price offer for you."

"That is good news," I say but I feel a pinch of sadness in my chest. My brain fills with memories of the day I got the keys to my two-story loft overlooking the ocean in Sydney. It was an indulgence I could make, and did, with pride. Of course Eric said he'd pay half the mortgage but then his mom needed help—so he said—and I dropped the rent for him from half to a fourth, but he only managed to pay that every couple of months. I still got by because my business was thriving, but it was a little bit tighter than I'd anticipated. But when I was enjoying weekend coffees or evening nightcaps overlooking the harbor it felt worth it.

"Stop," Cordy says, because she's always been able to read my thoughts. "It's just an apartment. There'll be others. And you don't even live here anymore."

She's kind of right, but I object anyway. "Australia will always be my home. I'm going to be back. A lot."

"And you can stay with me. Or, you know, those people who spawned us." She's smiling at her own joke. I can hear it in her tone. "You could stay there and they might not even notice. I don't think they even go into the East wing anymore since Mom moved her craft room into your old bedroom."

I scrunch up my nose. "Why did she do that again? I mean, shit, the house has five guest rooms and a guest house. And your room. Why did she have to take over mine?"

I'm acting sweaty and petulant, like an over-stimulated child at the beach, which should be embarrassing but I've got all this pent-up energy from making out with Gabriel and nowhere to put it. There's a pause from my sister, probably because she's rolling her eyes in response and forgets I can't see her.

"She told you, something about morning light or the fact that you can see the Big Dipper from your skylight. I don't fucking know." She sighs. "But what I do know is that I've sold your place. You're free. And you have to stop taking everything so personally. Especially with Mom and Dad."

"He hired Eric."

The silence is longer this time and I know it's because even

Cordy can't smooth over the horrible truth of this. "Okay, that is fucked up. And for the record, I've told him. Repeatedly. But he defends it to me the same way he defended it to you. He needs to work with someone and you would never work with him."

"So he hires my ex? The one he never liked to begin with? The one who stole my business going? That's who he hires to do PR for his new indie movie? The person who is the reason I'm selling my damn home?" I am pseudo-yelling. I don't yell. I am immediately mortified.

And then it gets worse when there's a faint knock on the door. I freeze. Oh fuck, am I getting a noise complaint? I turn and stare at the door with wide eyes and a thumping heart, like I know it's Jason Voorhees on the other side or something. "Pumpkin? Hello? Tell me you want to know the second good news?"

"I have to go," I mutter as I lean into the peephole and see a bellhop standing there.

"But I—"

I hit end on my sister shove my cell into my pocket and swing open the door. The bellhop looks at me and his muddy colored eyes flare. Right. I'm shirtless. "I'm here for your luggage, Mr. Walsh."

"Right. Now? Fuck." His eyes get even bigger. "Sorry. Umm... give me a minute."

I scurry about the hotel room making sure everything is packed that needs to be packed, but I leave out a new shirt and some fresh undies. I don't have to be down to the lobby for the car to the airport for another twenty minutes. They're just taking our bags ahead of time. So I open the door because it closed in the bellhop's face, and hand him the bag. "I'm just gonna take a shower real quick before check out."

He nods, like he gives a shit, which of course he doesn't. Then he leaves and I fly through the shower. I packed my deodorant and hair product but luckily this is a five-star and I can make do with the free toiletries in the room, which include a gel and some overly stinky deodorant.

Forty minutes later as I'm walking onto the small, luxurious private jet, I wonder why I bothered with a shower. Because I take one look at Gabriel who is sitting, ankle on knee, in a white leather chair and I'm overheating again. He smiles up at me from under his thick sandy lashes. I pretend not to notice and take the chair at the very back, three rows behind him so I can't be tempted to drool over him all flight. Of course, that doesn't stop me from thinking about him, and our sauna kiss, the entire time.

REGRET HAS BEEN gurgling in my gut the entire flight. So when we're finally able to get off this tin can, all I want to do is leave Axel and everyone else in my rearview and get somewhere where I can be alone. I went too far, too fast with Axel in that sauna. I was the guy that I keep telling him I'm not. The aggressive, selfish, arrogant prick who can't see boundaries to save his life.

As soon as the doors open, I'm on the tarmac. My father is calling after me, in French, so I turn and look back at him. But I don't stop walking. I make a point of keeping my sunglasses on so no one sees my eyes bounce from my father to Axel, who is walking a few feet behind him, to my father again. "You're forgetting something!"

"What?" I ask, trying not to sound so annoyed. But seriously, I have my messenger bag and my trainer, Enzo, beside me. The bags get delivered to the hotel so what the hell else do I need?

"*Votre copain, mon coeur.*" My boyfriend. Right. Fuck. Dad is smiling, but there's a hard glint in his hazel eyes that says 'don't you dare talk back' so I don't. I just nod, stop walking, and wait for Axel to catch up.

His step falters when he hears the exchange and sees me stop. Fuck, that regret gurgles and crawls its way up my throat, like acid reflux. Dad sighs. "I've arranged a nice meal for you to share together. Alone. At *Mon Ami Gabi* tomorrow night. Simple. Elegant. People Magazine might have been tipped off. Also Just Jacob."

"Just who?" I ask.

"I think you mean Just Jared," Axel says to my father so quietly I almost don't hear him.

Dad nods and then makes a flamboyant shooing motion with his hands. "Go. And do not mess this up, Gabriel."

He hasn't warned me like that since I was fourteen, and I've done a lot of shit that's deserved a warning in my life since then. That's how I know my dad has stopped with his version of gentle meddling and is in his full-metal meddling mode now. I stand perfectly still and let him pull me in to kiss both cheeks before he pats my shoulder and then turns and shakes Axel's hand.

"Enzo, you'll ride with me," Louis tells my trainer.

Axel and I walk side-by-side, as awkwardly as two men can walk, to the waiting darkened SUV. Heat shimmies off the pavement around us. Vegas is the Devil's armpit, I think, and wonder why of all the places they added this one to the calendar last year. Why not something somewhere that doesn't make my skin damp in a way I can't even pretend is dewy.

Once we're in the back of the SUV and the driver is pulling away from the private airfield, Axel pulls up his phone and stares at it like it's the secret meaning of life. Fine if he wants to ignore me, I can ignore him too. That lasts ten minutes. Then, because the gaudy scenery of obscenely large, shiny hotels and casinos outside is giving me a headache, I stare at him.

Merde, tension makes him attractive. His jaw muscle flexes absently and he occasionally rakes his teeth over his bottom lip as he scrolls on his phone. I fight the memory of how I once tugged on that plump lip with my own teeth. Just hours ago.

He must feel either the weight of my thoughts or my gaze, or both because his dark, brooding eyes flit up to meet mine. "What are you doing?"

"Looking at the menu for this restaurant we have to eat at tomorrow," Axel replies. "They're not big on greens."

"Greens?"

"Yes. You know, vegetables. Lettuce. Salad." He drops his phone into his lap as it pings, ignoring it. "I was hoping for a light dinner and an early night."

"We're in Vegas. A city built on sin and debauchery, and you were hoping for an early night and some salad?" I say, hoping he understands how utterly ridiculous that sounds when he hears it from someone else's mouth.

He considers it but shrugs. "I'm not used to this schedule. We're moving to another time zone before my body regulates to the one I'm in. Billy said it would be hard, but I didn't believe him."

Okay. I didn't consider that. He's right, the travel part of this can be grueling. Now I feel bad I didn't consider that this was all so new and difficult for him. I take a few long slow breaths, searching for a way to lighten the mood and make him happy. Two things that seem to be polar opposite ideas. "I think they have a wedge salad. You can get it with a vinaigrette instead of blue cheese if you want to ruin a perfectly good salad made by a gifted chef."

Something flickers across his face that resembles embarrassment. Not the good kind he gets when I'm propositioning him either. My humor isn't funny to him. Fuck. "Sorry. That was bitchy. You don't deserve bitchy."

"It's fine," he says.

"When a woman says 'it's fine' I've been told that it means my life is in imminent danger," I reply and his eyes, which had moved to the window, quickly move back to me. "I don't know if that's the same with men. I've never dated one so I'm unclear."

"You're not dating one now."

"No. I'm not in real life, but I am for People Magazine and Just Jacob," I reply and that gets me the faintest, quickest flash of a smile. Enough of one that my own lips turn up and relief starts to loosen the tension in my shoulders. "And while I'm apologizing I would like to offer one for my behavior in the sauna. I shouldn't have pushed."

"Pushed what?" Axel looks out the window again. "My buttons?"

"Yes. The sexual buttons," I clarify as my fingers twist in my lap. "I like to go after what I want, and I feel this energy with you that makes me... well, feral. And so I push. But I apologize."

"I kissed you, Gabe. Not the other way around."

Something in me disregards his words because that regret is still bubbling in my gut. "I know my behavior makes it seem like I am, in fact, the type of guy who gropes women on planes without their consent. But I'm not. And I guess I just finally understand that I need to walk the walk and not just talk the talk."

"You're *supposed* to grope me," Axel replies. He shifts a little in his seat so his lean torso is twisted to face me. "And you need to if we're going to get people talking. So let's just... sell it. Hard."

"There are too many damn double entendres in this arrangement," I mutter and for once, I'm the one blushing. Or at least I think I am. It's been so long since I've blushed... wait a minute, have I ever blushed?

Axel laughs. It's his first real, unbridled laugh around me.

It's a throaty sound with a rasp to it that makes my dick stir. The car stops in front of the Four Seasons, which is actually just the top half of Mandalay Bay. "I'll make sure your bags make it to you immediately."

I nod at the driver as Axel thanks him. A concierge is waiting at the front doors to greet us with a giant smile. Even before being a Formula One driver, this type of service was my life, but it's clearly not Axel's because he looks slightly uncomfortable as the concierge fawns over us and rambles on about amenities and guest services as she walks us to the elevators.

We chug up, alone in the metal box, both of us avoiding eye contact again. We're not only staying on the same floor at this hotel, we're in suites next to each other. Convenient. "So..." I clear my throat. "What are your plans tonight?"

"Eat. Sleep," he grunts out and then yawns. "Please don't dive head first into that sin and debauchery you say this town was built on. I don't need a new scandal to fix in the morning."

"I was going to go down to the lobby and play a round of Craps, naked, with a hooker on each arm, but I guess you're telling me that's a no-no?" He slowly turns his head to look at me and I blind him with a bright and innocent smile.

"You are your own worst enemy."

"I know. Believe me," I assure him.

We walk down the hall together. His room is the first one we hit. Mine is a foot away. I barely make it that foot when he says, "In the car you said you've never dated a man. Why?"

I shrug. "Never wanted to. Don't get me wrong, the sex is great and the conversations are easy. I just haven't felt a strong enough connection to pursue any of the men I've had sex with."

"What about dates. Just, like, first dates?" I must look as confused as I feel because he continues to explain himself. "You meet someone, they interest you. You ask them for coffee or dinner or a movie and you get to know each other. Before the sex part."

His description conjures up a whole bunch of scenarios I've seen on television, in movies, and read in books. But nothing I have actually experienced. I shake my head. "Nope. Never done that."

"You've never gone on a date?"

"Not with someone I haven't already seen naked, no." He looks positively dumbstruck. Maybe I should feel embarrassed about that but I don't. "I guess you're going to be my first date."

"I guess so," Axel says, awe still gripping his features in the cutest expression. He's all wrinkled forehead and wide eyes.

"See you at dinner tomorrow night." I press my key card to my hotel room door and twist the handle.

"Yeah. I'll knock on your door when I'm ready to go." Axel gives me another one of those brief flashes of a smile. "Be wearing more than a towel or bathrobe this time."

He slips into his room before the laugh even escapes my lips. As I step into my suite, I tell myself that we're good. He's cool with me, and I'm going to be cool with him. Even though cool is something I've never been.

I GOT my wish last night. I ordered a Chef's salad from room service and was in bed by ten. Jerking off to thoughts of that sauna kiss, but still. It was an early night. Then I got to sleep in. Gabriel had a series of work events—a photo shoot for a sponsor, an interview with an F1 podcast, and a segment to film for Sky Sports with his teammate Sterling. He was busy with his trainer and a team meeting in the afternoon, so I researched Allard Couture UK, making notes on the events they held and attended last year, what their social media is like, and what Influencers promote them. And then I went over the contract Cordy (now Delia) emailed me for the sale of my loft. I ignore the line in her email that says 'I still haven't told you my second piece of good news!' I love my sister but it's going to be something like "I've found a new favorite nail polish color that goes perfectly with my business cards." Or something equally as absurd. Or something about my parents, who I'm currently kind of mad at. Anyway, my day was good. And I was feeling a little bit more like myself.

But tonight... tonight isn't going to be an early night. I come to terms with that the second Gabriel emerges from his hotel room. He's dressed in a simple V-neck shirt in a muted salmon color and gray linen pants. I feel suddenly very formal in my button-down shirt. Thank God I opted to forgo a tie. I'd thought about it, like the clueless dickhead I am. I don't know why I thought fancy would be better in a slutty town in the desert. Jesus, you'd think I was raised by dingoes in the outback and not by a film icon in a swanky mansion in Byron Bay. Something about Gabriel throws me off what little game I've managed to develop over the years.

I'm still berating myself for almost wearing a tie as we enter the restaurant. But when he slips his hand into mine it pulls me out of self-disparaging thoughts, like a record scratch. When I swivel my head to him, his inky eyes are, for the first time since I've met him, uncertain. "You said go hard, remember?"

I nod and swallow and try to smile, which probably makes me look like I'm on the verge of a seizure. At least that's what I'm guessing from the furrowed brow of the host as he motions at our table, next to a plate glass window in the middle of the restaurant. Subtle, Louis, I think sarcastically. I clear my throat. "Actually do you have something... tucked into a corner? A booth or something less... see-and-be-seen?"

That's a PR term I shouldn't be using, but then again fuck it. When the press gets a hold of my name they'll know what I do for a living. If they find out I used shop talk with the maître d it wouldn't be a red flag. And they *will* pay the guy to spill his guts. They always do. He gives me a pleasant smile. "I can arrange that. How about this?"

I tug Gabriel along by our joined hands to follow the host past the window, in between a row of four-seater tables and a set of two-seater booths, to the back left corner of the place. He motions to the last booth on the wall there. I nod and smile and slip him a ten for this trouble. I let go of Gabriel's hand, my fingers tingle from the lack of touch in protest. Gabriel slips into his side of the booth first and as I slide into mine, he leans forward, tanned forearms on the table cloth, and whispers. "Shouldn't we have stuck with the plan and sat at the most prominent table in the place?"

Before I can answer that question, a spark illuminates behind those blue eyes of his and he flashes me those perfectly white teeth. "Ah. Wait... better if we seem like we aren't seeking out the attention. We're just there for us. Smart. You aren't just a pretty face."

I grin. He winks. The waiter, a twenty-something named Fred, introduces himself and tells us the specials. Gabriel orders a bottle of a red I've never heard of and two appetizers, a warm Brie with baguette and a large garden salad with extra veggies, Dijon vinaigrette on the side. Something in the center of my chest blooms like night jasmine, fragrant and sweet. He remembered I wanted salad and made it happen.

"Thank you," I say gratefully when the waiter leaves.

Gabriel waves a hand lightly and leans back in his chair. "Don't thank me for salad. Thank me for the wine, though, after you fall in love with it. And you will. It's French, luxurious and delicate all at the same time."

I bite back the urge to say something coy like 'so are you' because I don't think I could pull it off. Being flirtatious and cheeky is Gabriel's superpower, not mine. It might lighten the mood, though, and so I almost say it. Because something has been off with Gabriel since the sauna kiss. I wanted him to take this more seriously, but I'm regretting that now. This feels wrong. He's too serious and too quiet.

After a few tedious moments of silence, and the waiter uncorking the wine, which Gabriel tastes and approves, I pick up my glass, swirling it absently, and take a small sip. I don't normally like red wine... except this is fucking good. Not bitter, or heavy like most reds. This is exactly as he said—luxurious but delicate. "Thank you for the wine pick. You're right. I'm impressed."

"I can do more than drive fast and push your buttons," Gabriel replies as he sips his wine.

"You also do a shockingly accurate impersonation of a waiter on a yacht," I say and his eyes widen and a smile tugs up the corners of his mouth.

"And you have a cheeky bastard side to you. Who knew?"

I chuckle under my breath. "Okay so let's see what else we know about each other. Let's play two truths and a lie."

I don't know when I decided to be a fun guy, but yet, here I am. I've never played two truths and a lie with anyone. Ever. My sister told me about it when it was used as an icebreaker at a real estate conference or some such nonsense. I explain the rules to Gabriel, who is looking at me with a curious but baffled expression. We each tell each other three 'facts' about ourselves. Two are true and one is a lie and the other person has to guess the lie.

"I think I like this," Gabriel says and there's a glint of excitement in his eye as he leans forward.

We don't start until after the waiter has delivered our appetizers and asked about a main. Gabriel keeps his eyes on me as he tells our server, "We'll share the filet mignon. Medium, with peppercorn sauce, and asparagus instead of potato."

I give my head the slightest shake. Gabriel catches it. "Make that almond green beans. Not asparagus. *Merci.*"

We don't address the fact that he orders for us without asking or that he reads my gentle cues and pivots without an explanation. We both just lean forward and dip into the appetizers. I lay my linen napkin, the color of an evergreen, across my lap and pick up my fork. "Do you want to go first?"

Gabriel picks up a piece of the baguette and as his eyes drop to the melting brie dusted with cranberries and thyme, he speaks. "I'm allergic to peaches. I've fucked another driver currently racing in F1. I once had a cat named Edith Piaf."

See? This is why I don't try to be fun. Because it ends up not being fun. I'm going to have to wonder for the next several weeks maybe months, about which guy he fucked. Now I'll spend my spare time staring at each of the other drivers trying to figure out who got what I didn't have the balls to take when it was offered—a night with Gabriel.

Gabriel smiles cheekily as he waits for my guess. I swallow down a bite of salad and reach for my wine again. "I've never heard of anyone being allergic to peaches, but I assume it's possible. I also know, from my extensive research on Allard Couture, that Louis Allard is allergic to cats and dogs. Extremely. So that's the lie."

Gabriel doesn't say anything at first and he has quite the poker face so I can't read him but of course I'm right. Finally, he says, "What driver do you think I fucked?"

"I'm trying not to think about it," I admit and refuse to move my eyes off the salad. If I look him in the eye, I'll turn redder than the wine. "I mean, there are a lot of options. Rivera. He's smoldering hot and has a sexy accent. Grady Lewis? He's super cute and you and him are buddy-buddy in the interviews I've stumbled across. For research."

"For research, of course," He nods and a smug smirk appears, then disappears. "Grady is one of my only friends on the circuit. Great guy. But no, I haven't fucked him."

I gently pour some vinaigrette over the greens, focusing on it like it's the most taxing thing I've ever had to do. And then, like the fool I am, I keep talking. "Nord. He's a prince. Of course it was Nord. Who wouldn't fuck a prince?"

"Me," Gabriel says flatly and I finally dare to look at him. He shrugs. "First of all I had zero clue Nord was gay and I Karted with him for years when we were younger. Also, he's not my type. Too blond and too proper. I like guys with darker hair and darker eyes who act all uptight but come apart eventually. Like in saunas or on a yacht at midnight."

I nearly choke on a carrot.

Gabriel dunks a chunk of baguette into the creamy, oozing cheese and then into his perfect mouth. He makes me wait as he chews and swallows. "There are female drivers too. Samantha and Lucia. I'm bi, remember?"

"Okay so was it Samantha or Lucia?"

"It was Edith Piaf," Gabriel replies and I can't stop my face from scrunching up awkwardly in confusion. If People or Just Jared are snapping a photo right now, it probably looks like I sucked on a lemon or smelled a fart. Great. "Edith is a cat. I had a cat once."

My shoulders drop slightly in relief. He catches it. I can tell by the smile on his lips. He likes that I'm relieved. "I found the scraggly little calico under the porch of our summer house in Saint Jean de Luz when I was eleven. She was a sad, needy little thing and I knew that my father would gladly take her to a shelter if I told him about her, but I was also a sad, needy little thing that summer."

Oh, my heart.

"Dad was dating a new guy at the time. New relationships always sucked up a lot of his time. And he was launching the luggage line, so he was particularly distracted that summer. So instead of telling him, I just kept her. Under the porch at first, giving her blankets and food and water. I even got the cook to buy me some flea medication so I could get the bugs off her. And then when we got a few days of hard rain and low temperatures I was beside myself. Worried about her out there, alone and cold and wet, so I snuck out there in the middle of the night and took her to my room. My room became her room. She'd jump in and out of my window which was thankfully on the ground floor, and I'd sneak her around the house when Dad was out. She slept in my bed, or under it, or in my closet for six weeks. Ask Louis about the worse-than-normal allergies he had that summer. He blames climate change, but it was Edith Piaf. I named her that because Piaf was my dad's favorite French singer and this cat's purr reminded me of her gravelly voice."

"Why only six weeks?" I ask as he holds up a piece of baguette with cheese clinging to it and offers it to me. I lean closer and open my mouth and he pops it in. It feels somehow erotic even though I don't think he means it that way. "Did you get caught? Did she end up at a rescue?"

"She ended up under the maid's tire. Total accident," Gabriel replies. "I cried like I'd lost a parent, which baffled my father as he thought it was just a random stray. Now your turn."

He says it like his story didn't just break my heart. It did. I can picture sad, needy young Gabriel losing his only furry little friend and the ache in my chest is overwhelming. He loses the twinkle in his eye and says with an undertone of seriousness, "Don't. It's okay. I am over it. Mostly. Now please, your turn."

I sigh and try to shake off the sadness. "I'm scared of heights. I grew up with an Oscar on the mantle in our living room. My sister's middle name is Black-Heart."

Okay, that was a lame bunch of info, but I'm really bad at this. I hate sharing personal information with anyone. Gabriel has stopped eating and is just staring at me with a narrowed gaze like he's trying to use a Jedi mind trick to see into my soul for the right answer. "First of all, your sister's middle name isn't a fact about *you*."

"Yes, it is. Sort of. My parent's horrible naming skills affect my life too," I argue and he lifts a lone eyebrow in rebuttal. I surrender. "Fine. Whatever. How about... I'm scared of heights. I grew up with an Oscar on the mantle in our living room. I own a small cattle ranch in the outback."

Gabriel has time to think about it because the waiter swings by to clear our finished appetizer plates and put the steak down, with two plates and fresh cutlery. When he's gone I realize that salad was definitely not enough food. My mouth is watering as I look at the steak so I dive in without waiting, cutting off a chunk and popping it into my mouth. It's incredible and I let out a little groan.

Gabriel laughs. "Well, you are definitely not a guy who could devour a steak like that if you owned cows. You're too sensitive. You're... what is the English term? Bloody heart?"

I swallow down the steak and cover my mouth with my napkin as I laugh. "Bleeding heart?"

He nods, his sandy hair tumbling across his brow and into his eyes. He pushes it back absently. "Yes. That's you. You may eat meat but you couldn't raise it and kill it. You'd blame yourself for each cow's death like you seem to blame yourself for everything. So, no. You don't own a cattle ranch because you wouldn't be eating the steak with such *joie de vivre*."

"You're right." But *ouch* with the personality analysis.

"Reward me," he says as I cut a second piece of steak. He puts both elbows on the table, leans in, and as I hold out the steak on the end of my fork, he wraps his lips slowly around it. And just like that, I'm getting hard.

Sliding his lips, and the morsel of meat, off the fork, he leans back and chews. "Do tell me more about the Oscar."

"Uh... right. Well, I didn't win it, obviously," I sputter out and reach for my wine again, which thankfully the waiter topped up when he delivered the main. After a hearty sip, I continue. "My father won it. There are actually two on the mantle now. Like book ends. But I was in college when he won the second so I've never lived with it."

"Who the hell is your dad?" I can see Gabriel's mind

working overtime, probably flipping through every Australian actor he can think of.

"Dominic Hemming. Won for best director when I was seven and again when I was nineteen. Also, he has two Emmys from his work in television, but I thought if I mentioned those it would be so specific you'd know."

"Dominic Hemming?" Gabriel repeats and recognition covers his handsome features. "He actually deserved those awards too."

"Yeah, he's brilliant." I nod because, like it or not, it's true. And to be honest I don't not like it. I'm proud of my dad. "And yes we have different last names. I use my mother's last name professionally. Keeps people from wanting things from me I can't deliver. Like his attention. I can't tell you the number of people who slipped screenplays under my dorm door in college."

"I bet I got just as many sketchbooks from eager design students shoved under mine," Gabriel counters. "For the seven months I attended anyway, before I convinced my dad I didn't need higher education, I just needed to drive."

"I guess we have that in common. People using us to get close to our fathers."

Gabriel smiles, but it's a completely different smile than I've ever seen on his stunning face. It's real and candid and vulnerable. He's letting his guard down. The guard he cloaks in brashness and sarcasm. I feel a wave of victory, but also something else. I'm bonding with him too.

He cuts himself a piece of steak and then pops it in his mouth. After he swallows, he leans back. "I guess there was no way in hell you'd go into filmmaking even if it interested you."

"No way in hell," I confirm. "And it *did* interest me. Still does. A lot. But I create stories another way. Through the power of twisting the media narrative, which let's face it, is probably harder."

Gabriel drops a hand over mine on the table. A simple, easy gesture that fills my veins with gasoline and then he lights that gasoline with a smile. "I don't know. You are making it feel pretty easy."

I GAVE Axel the greens he wanted but not the early night. We stay at *Mon Ami Gabi* until there's no one else there. We ordered night caps and lingered over them and a shared Crème Brûlée. We discover each other through this silly little game he introduced, which makes me laugh and also, in some cases, takes my breath away. I'm boldly candid with him, because what do I have to lose?

I tell him I want more pets, like Edith Piaf, but can't have one because of my schedule. I list all the pet rescues I donate to instead. I tell him about my favorite Christmas, which was spent in Canada when my dad was dating a Vancouver businessman named Gilles, and we did the holidays in Whistler. Fighting yet another unheard of blush, I admit that I was scared of moths and butterflies as a kid and still prefer not to be around them, but won't run screaming if I see one now like I used to.

Axel isn't as boldly candid with personal information as I am, but he's trying, which I can tell for him is a huge deal. He tells me about selling his loft. There's melancholy in his voice even though he says it makes sense and he doesn't want to live in Australia right now. He explains he hates surfing, and I tell him should get his Australian passport revoked, and he laughs and nods. Alternatively, and nonsensically, Axel loves snowboarding, which he admits is essentially the same thing as surfing. I learn he loves seafood but can't eat anything with eyes staring at him, so his lobster and shrimp and such need to be dismantled before it's served. I laugh at that and call him a bloody heart again.

We pile into the SUV just after midnight and I try to fight the despair in my chest that this night is ending. I've enjoyed it more than anything I've done in the last few months, including racing. Axel doesn't pull out his phone or ignore me or sit as far away as possible, but he does get quiet. I take a second to absorb the feeling of his knee gently bumping mine and then decide to keep the conversation going instead of sliding my hand up his thigh, which is what I really want to do.

"Is your sister's middle name really Black-Heart?" I ask.

"I thought you didn't want information that wasn't about me," Axel shoots back with a quirk of his mouth. God, I want to beg him to wrap those lips around my cock.

I shake the thought from my head. "Well, I guess I've decided that it kind of is about you because if she has that crazy of a middle name then you must have an absurd one too."

"Her middle name is Joan," Axel says but the smile on his lips says there's more to the story. "But my crazy former rock band groupie-slash-model mother did want Black Heart. As a nod to Joan Jett and the Black Hearts, which was her favorite group growing up. Dad talked her into Joan instead. Officially she's Cordelia Joan Sydney Walsh Hemming. Sydney is where she was conceived. Cordelia is because it's my mom's favorite character on *Buffy the Vampire Slayer*."

"*Mon Dieu* and I thought the French picked weird names," I mutter and pause before pushing. "And you?"

"Well, Dad was the absurd one when it came to naming me," he explains. "And Mom didn't deter him."

"I'm waiting," I prompt when he doesn't say anything else. He takes in a long, slow breath, and I add, "I can just have Damien give me your file."

"There's a file?"

"There's always a file when you work for my dad," I reply, and he lifts both eyebrows but doesn't ask anything more.

"Axel Jericho Maximus Walsh Hemming."

"Jesus."

"Yeah, I'm surprised he didn't add that too," Axel quips. "And I know you'll want the backstory so... Axel is because of Guns-n-Roses of course, with my mom being the former rock band groupie. She wanted it spelled without the e, exactly like lead singer Axl Rose, but Dad insisted on Axel with an E. Jericho is because I was conceived in Vancouver, Canada, while my father was filming a movie, and they were staying in a house on Jericho Beach. Maximus is his favorite character in his favorite movie, that he didn't make."

"Gladiator?" Axel nods and I laugh. "Your driver's license and passport must be seven lines long."

"Look who is talking Gabriel Louis Joseph Charles Allard."

"You know my full name?" I am, quite frankly, gobsmacked. It's not an appropriate response considering I've been tabloid fodder since birth.

"Since New Year's when I googled you," Axel confesses, leaning closer like it's a conspiratorial whisper about torrid things. "I fell down a rabbit hole like a teenage girl with a crush."

I feel the heat building in me crank up a notch. "You have a crush?"

Axel smiles shyly. It's a good look on him. He should do it more often. But then he pulls back a little, tucking back into his half of the seat. His knee no longer bumping mine softly. "Of course I *had* a crush."

His use of past tense is intentional and disheartening. But being the petulant bastard I am, I ignore it. "So why did you ghost me?"

He shakes his head and shifts his gaze out the window. I feel like I'm popping this nice intimate bubble we're floating in, and I hate it, but I have to know. "I didn't ghost you. I wasn't going to be the guy who gets all Mooney-eyed over a random hook-up and tries to make it something it wasn't."

I open my mouth, trying to find the words to explain to him that it wouldn't have been out of line. That I would have gladly accepted him into my life and welcomed the chance to see if he could be more than a random hook-up. Sure I would have gotten him naked that night but I also would have gotten his phone number and kept in touch had he not run off like Cinderella at midnight. But before I can explain that to him he adds a fact that has me swallowing my words. "And also, I got back together with my ex later that week."

Oh.

Now it's my turn to pull back a little, both emotionally and physically. I lean against my door and rub my fingers across my pants. "The guy who made you think so badly about yourself?"

"Yeah," Axel sighs, his eyes moving from my face to the window next to me. "It was a mistake. That wasn't our first break-up. Or our last. Our relationship made Johnny Depp and Amber Heard look stable and healthy."

"Well, you aren't selling me on the whole dating men thing." It's a joke. A bad one, but I don't know what else to do.

At least it gets Axel to focus on me again, this time with a trite smile. "You would never let someone fuck you over, repeatedly, the way I let him fuck me over. You're... smarter."

"I'm not," I insist. "I'm just not a bloody heart."

Axel huffs out another hard laugh, as this bloody heart thing becomes our inside joke. The SUV pulls into the drive of the hotel, and he puts on his business voice and turns to me before the car comes to a stop. "We might have been followed here and there'll likely be paps outside the hotel just because it's a race weekend so..."

He holds out his hand. I want to refuse it because that authentic intimacy between us is gone and this feels like a job again. I mean, it always was, but now it *feels* like one. But I know he's right and so I drop my hand in his and lace our fingers together. The heat ignites inside me again at the feel of his skin pressed to mine.

A Four Season's staff member pulls open the door on Axel's side at the same time someone opens mine, but I follow Axel out his side of the SUV, our hands still joined. We walk leisurely into the lobby, both of us thanking the doorman who opens the door for us. I don't look to see if we're being photographed, but I'm sure Axel is right and we are. So I stop just inside the doors, and his forward motion yanks my arm a little until he turns to see what the delay is.

Without a word, he takes two small steps so he's right there in front of me, so close I have to tip my head up a bit to maintain eye contact. "Thanks for tonight," I whisper, my voice rough with candidness. "I'm glad you were my first date. Even if, you know... it wasn't real."

And then I lean forward and press my lips to his cheek. I'm trying to be respectful and maintain a boundary. I've kissed a million people on the cheek. I'm fucking French. That's what we do. So to me, this is platonic. But then, before I can pull away, I feel his free hand cup my jaw as his fingers hold my face still. He moves his face. The stubble on his cheek gently rubs against my lips, until it doesn't. Until there's nothing against my lips except his.

The kiss is soft and teasing, his tongue sliding out to touch mine so lightly I almost think I dreamed it. And it's perfect. And I know, with a clarity that warms my soul, that *this* is our first kiss. Our first real one, where Axel knows me, and I know him, and we both want this. For real. This is real.

THE AWFUL TRUTH WAS, I was supposed to remain professional, but I didn't want to. So I kissed him. Because I could claim it was for the cameras, and I would, if anyone asked. But my heart knew it wasn't.

He kisses me back as gently as I'm kissing him, which I know isn't his nature. He's rough and dominant, passionate not subtle. So he's trying here, now, to restrain himself and somehow that makes it hotter. I can feel the quiver in his spine as I let go of his hand and press my palm to his back.

Finally, I take a step back and start to the elevator, he falls in line beside me. The doors open. We step in, just the two of us. He punches the button for our floor. We both retreat to lean against the back wall of the small square compartment as it glides upward. I fix my stare on the numbers above the door as they climb, like my blood pressure.

"That was... it was well played, and a smart move, and subtle but on brand," Gabriel says, and I hear him exhale. "And so fucking hot I've got a throbbing dick in my pants."

"Me too," I admit.

"Shame you won't let me do anything about it," Gabriel murmurs just as the doors slide open.

I follow behind him as we make our way down the long, straight hall. He stops at his door. I should stop at my own, but instead, I move past my door and stop behind him, like my feet just hit Krazy-Glu. I hear the softest click as his key card taps the door, releasing the lock. I watch his hand turn the handle and push the door like he's going to step inside and leave me there. But then he says, "Fuck it."

And he's turning, grabbing the front of my shirt in a fist and, thank God, he yanks me inside with him. The door has barely swooshed shut when he slams my back into the wall. He has one hand in my hair and one on my hip, pressing tightly into the curve of it below my belt.

His mouth is wanton, his tongue searching and needy and my mouth is willingly a refuge. I can't get over how good this feels. Better than the first time. Better than the sauna. That wasn't real. He was taunting me, not wanting me. This is *all* want.

He pulls my bottom lip between his teeth as he leans back. When he finally lets go his eyes are glassy and dark and he rasps, "I don't want to pressure you."

"The only pressure I have is in my pants," I blurt out, but don't have time to even blush about it because Gabriel is grinning and a chuckle bubbles up from his chest before he kisses me again.

I tangle my hands in his hair like I did that first night. It's so soft and thick and my fingers disappear into it on a wave of nostalgia. His hand slips from my hip to my belt and he starts undoing it. And I don't even think of stopping him. In fact, my brain is cheering him on like a cheerleader at an American football game.

His lips move to my ear and that dirty little mouth of his

kicks in. "I want to suck you off. It's been on my to-do list for too long. And when you disappeared I thought I'd never get to cross it off."

"Gabriel," I pant out his name as he lowers the zipper on my pants and palms my hard cock through my boxer-briefs. The pressure on my cock lightens, our eyes meet. I want to say something but I'm suddenly shy. And overwhelmed. But still eager so I cup the back of his strong neck—Jesus, F1 drivers have thick, muscular necks—and pull his lips to mine again.

My tongue barges into his mouth and my lips suck and pull on his bottom lip. I tip my hips, pressing my cock into his palm again. He grabs my shoulder with his free hand and holds me still. "I need permission. I'm bossy and pushy but I'm not... selfish or greedy. Consent. I need consent. Tell me you want to fuck my mouth"

"Gabriel Allard." My breath is shaky but my words are sturdy. "I want to fuck your mouth. Please. Now."

He's gone. Dropping to his knees, yanking my boxer-briefs down my thighs. He wraps a strong hand around my base and I swear to God the ground shifts beneath my feet as his lips brush my tip. My head falls back and makes a dull thud sound as it connects with the wall. My eyes flutter closed and my mouth falls open as his lips circle my cock and he slides down over the whole damn thing in one long, slow motion.

I let out a strangled groan. Gabriel's pace becomes relentless and I'm fighting my release within seconds. He knows it too, the glint in his eyes as he looks up at me from under his dark blond lashes is cocky. Heat climbs my neck, and he tugs roughly on my balls and that's it. It's over. I'm coming before I can even warn him. My whole body shakes during its own personal earthquake, and I grab him by his hair and try to pull him off, but he's not having it. He sucks down every drop of me until my knees are buckling and I'm slipping down the wall. I land in a limbless heap and realize through the haze of my orgasm that Gabriel has, at some point, tugged his own pants and underwear down his thighs and is jerking himself off.

I wrap my hand around his and join his efforts. Our lips crash together for the briefest, hottest kiss, which is salty with the taste of me. It ends as Gabriel groans into my mouth and ropes of his come land on my shirt and his thighs.

His head drops forward, his forehead landing on my shoulder. I turn my head and kiss his face just in front of his earlobe. "That was..."

There are a lot of ways I want to finish that sentence, but most of them are crazily vulnerable and completely romantic and, quite frankly, should send Gabriel running. So I pick the least bold of all. "That was worth the wait."

"See, that's where we differ," Gabriel says as he gracefully gets to his feet and pulls me up too. "The fact that we're so hot together just makes me angry we waited this long. You should have reached out sooner."

I'm trying to figure out how to respond to that, but Gabriel doesn't wait for a response. He pulls me by the hand and we both kick out of our pants and underwear and walk to the bathroom to clean up.

Five minutes later, with the endorphins cooling in our blood, and warm washcloths taking care of the mess we made, Gabriel speaks in such a quiet even tone I almost miss it. "So, this was consensual, right?"

"Of course," I reply, concern pulling my eyebrows together as I watch him wipe his rippled abdomen in the mirror. "I know I can seem a bit timid, but I have promised myself I won't be anyone's pawn again. If I didn't want it, it wouldn't have happened, Gabe. I swear."

He nods. "Okay."

He doesn't sound convinced but he flashes me a small, hesitant smile as he makes his way out of the bathroom and back into his suite. I start to put together the pieces on this. "Look, I get being a little worried. In fact, it says a lot about your character that you are hyper-conscious after what this woman has accused you of. But, dude, I signed an NDA the size of *War and Peace*. Also, don't forget I made out with Waiter Gabriel, and if I was in this to screw you over, I would have done it then."

"Instead you ran away," Gabriel mutters but flashes me another smile like he's joking, but his eyes say he isn't.

"I told you then I was in a bad place," I remind him. "I made a bad decision."

He stops as he's pulling up his pants, which he retrieved from the floor. He tips his head to look over his shoulder at me. "You regret not contacting me?"

"Yes." The word leaves my mouth without a moment's hesitation. If I hadn't been such a timid bitch about the whole thing, I wouldn't have gotten back together with Eric. Maybe I would have been with Gabriel this whole time. Maybe I'd still own my damn company. But I'm not about to admit any of that to him. This isn't... it's not real at the moment and all of that is way too honest for a fake arrangement. So instead I walk over, tug on my own pants, and grab his jaw, pressing my lips to his. "I especially regret it now that I know what I was missing."

"You ain't seen nothing yet," Gabriel whispers against my lips.

And just as our second kiss starts to deepen there's a knock on the door. It's soft and faint, but it startles us both and we pull apart. Gabriel's eyes flash with something that looks a bit like both guilt and recognition. "Oh fuck."

"Oh fuck?"

He walks over to the door, holding up a finger at me as if to say 'just a sec'. He cracks the door, barely. "Hey. I forgot to text. This isn't a good night."

"Really? But we…"

"Sorry," he cuts off the confused female voice. "I can't tonight. Right now. I've got… a lot going on."

"Isn't that the point of seeing me?" the voice asks.

Oh God, I do not want to be here for this. I run my hands through my hair and begin to pace as he whispers something I purposely avoid hearing. I debate sticking my fingers in my ears and chanting 'I'm not listening. Blah, blah, blah' like a five-year-old.

He closes the door and turns back to me. Our eyes lock and I clear my throat. He opens his mouth to say something but I hold up a hand. "I don't need an explanation. I'm not owed anything, Gabriel."

"We're back to Gabriel?"

"Huh?"

"You started calling me Gabe tonight."

That's a shift that I guess means something to him. I feel bad I've taken it away, but after what I just heard I realize I need to distance myself. I can't be that same idiot who falls for every guy that gives him attention. Look where that got me last time. "Gabe, I should go."

"It's not the same when you say it like that," Gabriel says, almost pouting.

"Look, I had a great time tonight. I don't regret a minute of it," I admit and give him a smile I hope doesn't look awkward. "I just… we need to keep in mind what we're doing and why. And if you are having extracurriculars with someone… whoever that was… then I'm keeping this… professional. I hope you get it."

I walk to the door and smile at him again as I leave. But he's not smiling back. "It's late. We'll talk tomorrow."

And I leave like I guess I always do with Gabriel.

DAD IS BEAMING when I walk into the cafeteria at the paddock. Back-to-back race weeks are always a grind. I mean, I love what I do, but it's a lot with the travel, physical endurance, and mental gymnastics involved. And now we've added fake dating to the itinerary, which apparently I'm better at than the rest of the things. I try not to think about that so I don't get depressed.

Dad holds up his phone screen. I see a picture of me and Axel kissing in the lobby of the hotel last night. Above it the headline "Gabriel Allard Comes Out with Mystery Man."

I roll my eyes. "I've been telling anyone who would listen I'm bi since I was fifteen."

"I know *mon coeur*, but visual confirmation is always more meaningful to the masses." I drop down in a chair across from him and pull out my phone, Googling my name. Yep. The first five links are all stories about how I'm suddenly gay. I swear under my breath, but I scroll through all of them as my trainer drops a well-curated plate of food and a chai latte in front of me.

I have to admit, I like the pictures of Axel and me together. Especially the ones in the restaurant. We look relaxed and happy. He's mind-blowingly pretty when he smiles. Not a word most men want to be called but I can't help but use it. He's got eyelashes for days and the way that pink color conquers his high cheekbones when he's being shy is just amazing. I screencap one of the better photos and immediately make it the wallpaper on my phone screen.

"Are you listening?" My dad's voice pokes through my reverie.

"No."

"Gabriel, you are going to have to keep your cool with the press today," Dad warns me. "You can remind them your sexuality was never a secret but do it politely. And it wouldn't kill you to smile a little if Axel's name comes up. Did you rehearse some facts about him? So this is believable?"

"Well let's see... I know his full name, his sister's full name, the fact he hates surfing but loves snowboarding and that his dad has won an Oscar," I rattle off. Internally my brain adds, *and I know how his cum tastes.*

"His dad won a what? An Academy Award?" Dad asks, eyes wide.

"Yeah. His real last name is Hemming. His dad is the director, Dominic Hemming," I explain and lean forward. "You didn't know that?"

"I did," Damien interjects as he sits down next to my dad with a plate of eggs and bacon. Fuck, I wish I could eat bacon during race season but it's not on the list of approved foods. "He doesn't like people to know. Kid is trying to make his own way and all that noble garbage."

I pick up my spoon and dive into my Greek yogurt and granola parfait. My dad looks stricken and then he says, "I'm so glad you don't do that, Gabriel. I worked hard for our family name to mean something. I want you to use it with pride."

"I'll always proudly be an Allard, *Papa*," I assure and give him a smile as I keep eating my boring breakfast. I wonder though, if I would be in a different place if I had been like Axel and made my own way instead of always relying on the help my dad is overly eager to give. "Although you may wish I wasn't if we can't prove this woman's accusations are false."

"I would never wish such a thing, in any situation," Dad promises. "We will prove it, somehow, and even if we don't, know that I believe you, Gabriel. And I'm always going to believe you."

My dad leans forward and cups my face, his eyes shining with pride. And I remember, I'm not Axel. I wasn't created out of the love of two people, or even as a mistake between two humans and a night of passion. No, I was created because my dad wanted a child. I was this idea he willed into fruition, alone, with money and donor eggs and doctors. It may not be a normal attitude, but I can't help but feel a bit of pressure to never, ever hurt him because of that.

"There were cameras inside the plane, but they don't know if they were turned on," Damien announces. "The company you use for jet rentals rarely turns them on. In fact more times than not, they're off for passenger privacy. But they'll get back to me soon with confirmation. If they weren't turned on, we'll need to find another avenue."

"*Merde*," Louis swears under his breath. "Okay. Well, meanwhile this thing with Axel is providing the distraction we wanted. You two, with the kissing, really sealed the deal. Are you okay? Is he? With the fake affection?"

My dad is whispering now, his eyes darting around the cafeteria. No one is paying attention to us. A perk of being the driver no one takes seriously. I can't help but notice the crowded table where Sterling sits. The happy smiles on everyone's face who gets to share space with him.

"Yeah Dad, he's cool. I'm cool," I assure him, scooping up the last of my breakfast parfait. "Except I canceled an appointment with Dr. Jang last minute and I'm worried she won't rebook me."

"How last minute?"

"She knocked on my hotel room door," I say. Dad frowns. "I know. I honestly didn't think the meal with Axel would run so late."

Or that I would be sucking him off after dessert.

"I'll talk to her," Dad sighs. "You know she's the best damn acupuncturist in the United States. The fact that she agreed to fly out here to treat you at fucking midnight, is a big deal. Every rich person on the planet is lined up to see her."

"I will fit her into my schedule whenever today, I swear."

Dad stands, picking up his phone and typing. "This is going to cost more, I can feel it."

He walks around the table and lightly ruffles my hair. He's been doing that since I was a toddler and I love it. It brings me a sense of peace. "You just concentrate on saying the right things at the group presser this morning. I'll handle everything else."

"No one asks me questions at the pressers," I remind him, shoving away my empty parfait bowl and reaching for my latte, which is lukewarm now just like I like it.

"That's gonna change today, Gabe. Just you watch," Damien says.

"It's Gabriel," I remind him, but he's already lumbering off after my dad so he probably doesn't hear me. I lean back in my chair and watch them go, sipping my latte.

An hour later, I walk into the group press conference, which is done in packs with five or six drivers at a time. They mix it up, but generally, they try to keep the teammates in different groups. You never know what drivers will be in your group. I realize before we even begin, that Damien was very, very right about this presser being different. The public relations manager for F1 grabs my arm as I make my way to the end of the couch because I'm always on the end. No one wants me front-and-center and I give zero shits. Or at least that's what I keep telling myself.

"Not today," Holly says quietly. "You're sitting next to Cristian today."

"But... okay," I say like an idiot.

Cristian is in the middle of the long, curved couch. He smiles at me as soon as I sit down. Cristian's smile makes him look like he's got an inside joke you should know about, but don't. Our eyes lock and he says, "Welcome to the club."

"Club?" I blink.

"Ignore him. There is no club," Jasper Nord says, leaning over from his spot on the other side of Cristian. Jasper is always front and center too. He's not only Finnish royalty but also a driver who looks like a Ralph Lauren model and he wins. A lot.

Cristian laughs. "But if there was a club, we could have a secret handshake or something cool like that."

Jasper rolls his eyes and sighs like Cristian's on his last nerve. But his eyes are smiling as he watches Rivera laugh. Right. These two are gay. That's the club. And I'm in it now because of the kiss. Or more specifically, the media coverage of the kiss.

I just nod and smile and listen to Jasper and Cristian make small talk. It's more like bickering, honestly, but somehow I also feel like it might be foreplay. Finally, the reporters file in and sit down and Holly starts the conference.

They start with a guy from Sky Sports. He clears his throat. "My question is for Gabriel. I was wondering if you feel like you can hold the ground you claimed in qualifying last time, and maybe even do better here in Vegas? Also, you seem much more grounded now than at the beginning of the season, has anything changed, personally?"

I smile. Jesus, I guess no one is even going to try and be

subtle about this. I rub my palm on my knee and pretend to give the question serious consideration. "Well, I mean, I think Mayflower's engineering team has really worked out the bugs I was having with the engine. It felt so much smoother in Montreal and Miami. I expect the same here. As for the second part of your question, I feel I have enough races under my belt that I'm starting to get the hang of things at this level of driving. I'm in a much better mindset since I've settled down, personally."

"That picture—"

"Are you referring to the guy—"

"Is he your—"

"Okay kids, simmer down," Grady Lewis says into the second mic, which he's plucked from Holly. "You're acting like this is TMZ, not Formula One."

The room chuckles, albeit sheepishly. I look down the row at Grady, give him a smile and then hold up my microphone again. "I'm dating someone. His name is Axel. That's all you need to know. I've always been bi, this is not scandalous or news, sorry if you missed that sentence on my Wikipedia bio."

More chuckles so I smile and then I say, "Anyone else think this race is a bit of a lottery for everyone since it's a new track? I mean, anyone can win, right?"

That shifts the conversation and all the other drivers in my group—Christian, Jasper, Grady, and Spencer—all start bickering good-naturedly about who has an advantage. Holly manages to rein them all in again and the reporters get back to asking more questions.

There are a few questions for everyone else, but also a few more for me, which are remarkably on-point and about racing, not Axel. And not a mention of the accusation and potential court case. That feels like a miracle. And when it ends, it's the first presser I've enjoyed since I moved up from F2.

When I get up and the other set of drivers filters in to take our place I find Axel waiting for me. He's freshly showered in a crisp deep blue shirt and a pair of beige pants. He gives me a grin, which he tapers down immediately to a smile. Always buttoned down, that boy of mine, I think and I don't stop to correct myself on the ownership part, although I should.

"That was... Pleasant."

"Told you this would work," Axel replies and reaches up to squeeze my shoulder. "I know what I'm doing."

"I guess you do," I reply and drop my hand on top of his for a second. Because I want to feel his skin again. "Either that or you're just my good luck charm."

"I doubt that," he replies. "I have shit luck."

"I don't, not when you're around." I kiss his cheek impulsively and get the blush I love so much as a reward.

"Don't you have to get ready for your first practice?"

"Yup. But first I need to check with my dad to see if he managed to rebook my acupuncturist," I explain as I pull my phone out of the back pocket of my pants. "She was coming to my hotel room to help me with my wrists, which sometimes ache after races. But I kind of blew off the appointment."

"Your acupuncturist?" he repeats, the doubt on his face clearly visible.

"One thing you should know about me," I tell him as we walk out of the press building and into the glaring sun of Vegas at noon. We both slip our sunglasses from our hair to our eyes. "If I was going to lie, I would make it something much more entertaining and believable than an acupuncturist and sore wrists."

I hold up my phone, showing him the text I got during the meeting from my dad.

I had to pay double but Dr. Jang will be at your hotel, again, at three. Do not miss this or she might shove those needles of hers up my ass.

"Oh." Axel swallows and I watch his Adam's apple bob.

"It's okay. I get it," I reply and reach over and lightly rub my hand on his back in a consoling manner. But really it's to bring me comfort more than him. I like touching him. "But for the record, I agree. If we're going to do stuff to each other, even when no one is watching, then we do it monogamously. And I hope we do because last night was fun."

"It was." He turns that fabulous shade of sunburn again.

"I'm off to the garage," I tell him. "Stay close in case I need to rub your belly like a Buddha."

He laughs and turns off to go to the paddock. I walk to the garage feeling lighter than I have since this scandal began. Hell, since the season began.

Two LONG, sleepless nights later I haven't really seen Gabriel outside of the track. The night after our conversation he had a driver's dinner. I stayed in and made a pros and cons list about whether I should let things keep happening between us. And then tore it up when the cons seemed to be winning.

Last night, he was exhausted after press all day and a practice at dusk and that acupuncturist was seeing him again. I saw her, passed her in the hall, so I know she's real. Not that I doubted him because I've started to realize Gabriel is nothing if not authentic.

I went out to dinner with Billy and Frankie and after two hours of watching them be the perfect couple without even trying, I went home and picked apart every single moment of my six on-and-off again years with Eric, trying to find just one single moment of it where we seemed as in sync, at ease, and in love as Billy and Frankie. I couldn't find one. God, what a waste of my life that was. Then I thought of that one fake but real date with Gabriel and how it was easy and we felt in sync... then I let my brain relive the moments in his hotel afterward and jerked off to the memory in the shower.

So emotional turmoil, the constant dry air-conditioned air pumped into the hotel suite, and my jet lag left me a shell of a man. This is not how I want to be when Louis approaches me while I sip my latte on the balcony of the paddock.

Gabriel should be in the garage now, getting ready for his first qualifying round. I needed a minute before I walked over there. It's not uncommon for wives and girlfriends to be in the garage, especially during non-race sessions when the stakes aren't high and the team is just figuring out the track and the car on the track. Louis also isn't the only dad who shows up in the garage. Cristian Rivera's dad is there a lot, and Lucia Castera's dad is too. I won't be out of place. However, I have a feeling all the media will focus on is me because it's my first appearance since we've been 'outed' by the press. I'm ready for it, at least that's what I keep telling myself.

"I'm pleased," Louis says as he comes to a stop, leaning on the railing next to where I stand, his hazel eyes surveying the hustle and bustle below us. "I told you though, that there was no real intimacy required. Kissing, on the lips, is real."

"I know." I stare at the foam in my cup rather than Louis. If I meet his eye, I don't think I have the poker face to hide my attraction to his son. "It just felt right. And it was my decision, not Gabriel's. He has been a perfect gentleman about this arrangement."

"I believe you. Because I know my son, he may be bold and brash but he's not a predator," Louis reaffirms. "If I thought he did this, I would, as much as it would destroy me, hold him accountable. But I know he's not that type of man."

I nod. We've had this conversation, so I don't need to say much. I wish my father had the same unwavering love, pride, and trust for me as Louis has for Gabriel. My dad doesn't hate me by any means. He's never been cruel or even dismissive, but I'm like some puzzle he doesn't have the time or inclination to figure out. He's polite, and kind, but he's distant. I might as well be an employee.

"But did you... I mean, it's not my business but... when you left the lobby..." Louis pauses, his eyes darting from me back out to paddock row below us. He can't look me in the eye, which is astounding. This man runs a fashion empire, he's got the two biggest American racing tycoons under his thumb, and he can't look *me* in the eye. That says he knows this isn't his place. "Look, I just don't want this to be a French fry to oil... no I mean a fryer to pot... what the hell is that American expression?"

"Fryer to frying pan?"

He nods and smiles sheepishly. "Yes. I just don't want this to be a fryer-to-frying pan situation. Where we save my son from one problem by creating another."

"Mr. Allard... Louis. I won't be hurting your son's reputation in any way, for any reason." I turn to face Louis, leaning my arm on the railing.

"But I'm more worried about his heart with you." He turns to face me and a soft smile hits his mouth as he takes in the shock on my face. "He's different since you started this... project. He's got a *joie* I haven't seen in him in years. Not when he's out of a race car, anyway. And I know why you took this position. I'm the one who laid out the deal. You want a position in my company. You don't want a boyfriend."

"I think you're just being an overprotective dad," I assure him, trying not to let the entire tone of this conversation panic me, which it desperately wants to do. "Gabe and I were acquaintances before this arrangement, so there's an ease that comes with that. Your son isn't... he's all those things you mentioned—bold and brash—but he is also smart. He knows what this is. He's just not the type of person who does anything with less than one hundred percent, so he's giving this everything. We agreed we'd sell it, hard."

"You think?" Louis still seems skeptical. "I feel like he's never fully invested in anything. But he seems invested in you."

"I think he likes to act like he doesn't care about things sometimes," I reply. "But he cares."

I'm slightly uncomfortable talking about Gabriel with his dad. It feels like I'm breaching a trust, but I have to remind myself I'm employed by Louis, not Gabriel. I owe Louis, not Gabriel. Fuck, this is getting complicated. That's a red flag.

I clear my throat and take a final sip of my now cold latte. I pull myself off the railing. "We should head to the garage. See how he's doing."

The first roar of an engine on the track fills the air and Louis nods and walks with me. I drop my latte mug in the cafeteria, and we make our way in silence out of the paddock and to the garage.

Once there, I tuck into a corner to keep from bothering anyone. Mechanics and engineers are rushing about and Bob and Zack are seated in front of a monitor there, instead of on the row with the engineering director and others just outside the paddock. Louis doesn't feel the need to cower in a corner like I do. He struts about the place like he owns it because he kind of does. He walks over and plucks a set of headphones off a holder and stands in front of Zack, blocking his view of the monitor, to watch Sterling and Gabriel do laps.

I have no idea how it's going, but everyone seems pleased until they don't. Suddenly Bob and Zack both start swearing. The mechanics all drop their heads into their hands. An engineer jumps out of his seat and runs off somewhere. I pull myself up from where I was leaning against a wall and uncross my arms. My eyes find Louis, who is the only one not reacting.

I sneak myself over to the monitor to stand behind him and I see a Mayflower car in the wall. Pieces of red, white, and blue carbon fiber are scattered about the track. My heart leaps into my throat. "Gabriel?"

Louis shakes his head. "Samuels. That's why everyone's upset."

Oh.

"Is he okay?" I ask, and Louis nods again. My eye catches Samuels already on the other side of the wall, helmet tucked under his arm and a scowl on his face.

I retreat back to my corner, but I can't stop thinking about how worried I was. I mean, yes, it's normal to panic if you think someone you know might be injured but I was... well, the reaction was intense. And completely uncontrollable, which is a bit nuts.

When practice is over, and Gabriel's car is being moved into place in the garage, a few people walk over and high-five him as he pulls himself out. Louis is downright thrilled, wrapping his son in a big hug and slapping his back as he grins. So clearly Gabe did okay.

I slowly make my way over as he's tugging off his helmet and all his protective gear to expose his handsome face. He's grinning and he immediately turns his head to find me. And then I'm grinning. "It went well?"

He laughs and pulls me into a hug. "You didn't watch?"

"I didn't want to get in anyone's way," I say and as he lets me go I shrug.

"You make sure he gets a headset and a place to watch for qualifying, okay Dad?" Gabriel says and Louis nods. Then Gabriel looks at me again. "I had the second fastest time out there."

"That's incredible!" I say as my jaw drops.

"The car felt really great. I like the track. Tires had a little trouble at first because it's still really hot from the day but the actual race will be later at night so I think the grip won't be an issue and I'll have a better start."

Louis squeezes his shoulder again. An engineer walks over and turns to Gabriel. "Can you email me a breakdown of things? I have to go handle the Samuels situation."

"Yes. No problem."

I am clueless about this sport, which really makes me an idiot. I should have asked Billy more questions growing up. "So, I guess Samuels' crash was a pretty big deal if it's all hands on deck?"

Gabriel hands his gear to someone, his gloves, helmet, balaclava, and motions for me to walk with him. "No. It wasn't that bad actually. But they always focus on him. He's their star. I usually do my updates and debriefs with them via text or email."

"What?" I blink and he shrugs like it's no big deal. I let my eyes scan the garage now.

Both Bob and Zack are huddled together with Sterling in the corner by his mangled car. There's every mechanic in the place, except for two, working on Sterling's car. The void on Gabriel's side of the garage is more than noticeable.

"He doesn't need all their meddling anyway. He's doing fine," Louis announces and then starts asking Gabriel about the practice session.

I keep my mouth shut and follow along behind them. I have to keep reminding myself that this side of his life, the driving side, is not what I'm being paid to be involved in. I shouldn't care or even have an opinion on how he's working with his team. Or not working with them.

"I have to meet with Damien," I tell Gabriel and Louis as we make our way to the paddock. "Work stuff."

Louis nods and Gabriel shoots me a slightly disappointed glance but he nods too. "Dinner tonight?"

"Yeah. Sure." I am more excited than I should be about it.

He leans close and I press my lips to his cheek as he does the same to mine. I can't help but notice the camera crew in the distance. It's situated in front of Lighthouse Racing's paddock, shooting b-roll I assume as there's no driver in sight, and now they've turned the lens toward us.

I make sure my smile is bright, my gaze loving, as I wave goodbye and head in the other direction. It's easier to do than it should be. I realize I'm not acting anymore. I'm enjoying being Gabe's fake boyfriend. Another red flag starts waving in the back of my brain.

18 / GABRIEL

Dinner tonight isn't staged so I decide we'll kind of wing it. My plan is to wander the strip, check out some of the gaudy, ridiculous sights, and then find some food along the way. I don't know why, but just the idea of hanging out with Axel has me smiling. I mean, I do know why, and it's not just because I hope the night will end the way our last date did. Although, that's definitely got me smiling. It's just that I really like his company. I think he's fast becoming a friend. I haven't really had one of those, except Grady, in a long time. And the friends I have made in my life—mostly from school—have kind of drifted out of my life. It's hard to hold onto friendships when you're bouncing around the world for work eight months of the year.

I take my time getting ready, showering, shaving, and putting on extra aftershave. Picking out my outfit takes longer than normal too, which is stupidly simple—a pair of beige cotton shorts and a navy linen buttoned shirt with no collar and the sleeves rolled up to my elbows. And I toss on some navy leather running shoes from my dad's new shoe collection because we'll be walking a lot.

I had sent a text to Axel earlier and he said we'd meet in the lobby at seven, but by seven fourteen I feel like I'm being stood up. He's nowhere in sight. I text him and he doesn't answer, but I can tell he's seen the message on WhatsApp. I start to get annoyed.

I see Grady walk by and he stops. "Hey. What are you doing standing here?"

"I'm waiting for..." I take a beat. "My boyfriend."

He smiles. "You lose him on the walk from the hotel room to the lobby?"

Right. Of course people think he's staying with me. That's what boyfriends do. I laugh too but it comes out tight and fake because it is. "No. He's doing a work thing and was going to meet me here."

"Oh cool." Grady takes a step but stops and turns back to me. "I'm happy for you. Surprised, but happy. You never mentioned him or anything."

"I know. I just... I wasn't sure where this thing with Axel was going until... we just kind of got there." I run a hand through my hair, hoping my vagueness is acceptable. "And besides, you've been preoccupied with your team and stuff."

He grins a little at the word stuff. He knows I mean his boyfriend Ben.

"Okay well, I'm always here for ya, buddy," He claps my shoulder. "If you guys are going outside, good luck. I tried to go for a run out there, and I sweated off half my body weight. It's gross."

He disappears towards the elevators and then a hotel employee walks by and asks if I need help—directions or anything. I know he's just doing what he's told to do—take extra special care of a V.I.P. guest—but I feel more annoyed. Where the fuck is Axel?

Look, if you aren't coming, just say it. I look like
an idiot standing here."

I see the blue check that proves he's read it and for a second
it says 'Axel is typing' at the top but then it disappears and
there's no response. I swear in French and shove my phone into
my pocket. I march over to the elevators and am about to head
back to my hotel room to order room service and then call
Damien and fire Axel's ass when the doors to an elevator open
and he's in front of me. With Billy and Frankie beside him.

"Hey, mate!" Billy says with a grin as he steps out and cups
my shoulder. "We're tagging along for dinner. Axel said you
wouldn't mind."

I look over at Axel and he looks away as he steps out beside
Frankie. "Yeah. Sure."

Frankie leans over and we double kiss in greeting, which is
the standard way Europeans greet each other. None of this
handshaking, shoulder-clapping crap the Americans, Brits, and
Aussies do. "It will look like a double date if the press catches us.
And no one expects you guys to get all handsy in front of others,
so it takes the pressure off."

I'm staring at Axel so hard that he must feel it because he
finally looks up at me. He looks guilty as I say to Frankie, "Yeah.
Wouldn't want the pressure."

I turn to Frankie, swallowing the rejection and disappoint-
ment I feel over this, and give her a smile. "You have any
suggestions on what we can do? I've never been to Vegas
before."

"Oh honey, buckle up," she laughs. "I've got a ton of ideas!"

"My girl loves a good time," Billy says with a grin. Axel falls
into step beside his best friend and I walk next to Frankie, who
hooks her arm through mine like we're besties.

I have a feeling this might create even bigger rumblings in

the media since she's the Principal of another team. It's not uncommon for drivers to hang out together, but a Team Principal with rival drivers is not as common. "Nick and Lucia want to join us later too."

"Great. The more the better," I say but inside I'm having a hard time tamping down all the negative feelings.

Axel is avoiding being alone with me. And it makes me feel like I did when Edith Piaf got run over. Wounded and abandoned. I like him even more than I realized and that bothers me. A lot.

The night, if the circumstances were different, would be really enjoyable. Frankie and Billy are a hoot together. They banter and bicker and challenge each other every five minutes. But they're also incredibly handsy with each other and their chemistry radiates off them. Lucia and her boyfriend Nick are much the same. Only they're a little less competitive with each other and they look at each other with a softness that feels like you've walked in on something intimate every time you notice it. It just makes me jealous. I've never shared a look like that with anyone.

And also, this whole thing makes me feel a little lonely. Because I know these couples hang out together all the time, and being this social is part of their working life. I'm always alone in my hotel room if I'm not partying with strangers in random bars. I don't live like this during the season.

And a nagging part of my brain says they're only here with me tonight because they're Axel's friends. I wouldn't be invited otherwise. But still, it's nice to hang out with them. We walk the strip, taking in all the crazy sights and then we stop for dinner at Hell's Kitchen. Lucia is obsessed with the raving lunatic of an English chef and her British boyfriend Nick rolls his eyes the whole time but indulges her.

The food is good. Axel sits across the long booth from me, so

I can't touch him, which annoys me. He seems perfectly fine—friendly and jovial. He engages me in conversation like nothing's wrong, but something *feels* off.

After dinner, we stop and play some slots at the casino in Caesars Palace, at Lucia's insistence. "Come on! When in Rome... get it?"

She twirls with her arms extended, referring to the Roman embellishments all around the casino hotel. Her boyfriend smirks at her. "You want to bankrupt yourself? These things are rigged."

"The whole casino is not rigged," Billy replies. "But there's a reason the world isn't filled with blackjack millionaires or craps billionaires. Every casino game has a statistical probability against you winning."

"Killjoy," Frankie says and kisses his cheek before grabbing Lucia's hand and traipsing through the loud machines and tables with the sharply dressed dealers.

Axel follows along before everyone else, and I get the distinct impression it's to keep his distance from me, not so much his excitement at gambling. Maybe I'm taking this all too personally but it's hard not to. I felt like we were... really liked each other the other night.

Billy stays back, walking beside me. He shakes his head at his girlfriend and his teammate Lucia. "Those two will probably win hundreds. They like to defy odds."

"Really?"

"Well, Lucia was the first female F1 driver in decades, before Sam," Billy says and then winks at me. "And Frankie landed me, the hottest man in Australia who was sworn to a life of bachelorhood."

I can't help but laugh at that statement. I should have known it was coming with the wink he gave me. "What a lucky girl."

"Yeah, I mean, you're pretty lucky to be snagging the second-hottest man in Australia," Billy counters.

"We both know that's not exactly true," I mutter as the girls settle in at two slot machines. One called Wheel of Fortune and the other called Speed Chaser, which features a car. Of course, Lucia plops herself down at that one.

"Slots, on average, have the worst winning ratio of all casino games," Billy announces.

Lucia glares at Billy like he's being super offensive but Frankie grabs the front of his shirt and pulls him in for a kiss as she says. "You're much prettier when you're quiet. Now give me a kiss for luck."

Billy kisses her like she's the only person on the planet. And he couldn't be happier about it. I pull my eyes away before I puke rainbows or something. Their love is the kind that makes you lonely when you see it.

"You going to throw money down the toilet like my girl and her sister?" Nick asks as he comes to stand beside me.

"Nah. I was thinking maybe I would call it a night," I reply casually. My eyes are purposely on Axel who is standing half a foot to the left of me, close enough that I can catch his body tense when I speak. He heard me.

"If gambling isn't your thing, you're welcome to grab a drink with me at the bar," Nick offers.

Lucia hoots loudly, cutting into our conversation, and we all turn to see she's won a hundred dollars. She raises both arms in the air. "Yeah, bitches! Mama's buying new shoes."

What's hysterical is that Lucia has a million-dollar contract and was born into money, so a hundred bucks is like ten to her but she's clearly over the moon. Nick laughs at her and I turn to leave. I make it to the edge of the casino floor when a familiar touch lands on my shoulder.

"I don't see the point in me being here, Axel," I say without turning around. "You have fun with your friends. It's cool. I will see you tomorrow."

"Well, a pap followed us in here. He's from the Daily Mail or The Guardian, maybe? Something British judging by the Marks and Spencer T-shirt," Axel says and his mouth is so close to the shell of my ear that his breath tickles me. "He'll wonder why you left and I stayed. And besides that, I wanted these people to be more than my friends. I wanted them to be yours, so why not stick around and see if that can happen?"

"I don't need friends," I mutter like a spiteful child.

"We all need friends, Gabe," he whispers back.

He used Gabe. And he sounds so earnest. I am a sucker for authenticity. I close my eyes a beat and then turn around, heading back to the casino. I don't look at him, but I reach back, grab his hand, and take him with me to a slot machine a few feet from his friends. It's got a leprechaun on it and it's called Pot of Gold. I pull a crisp American fifty out of my wallet and push him down into the seat. As I feed the money into the machine I say, "You said you had no luck, prove it."

Axel laughs and tilts his head back to look up at me. His dark eyes dance and the smile on his face is breathtaking. My heart thumps a little harder in my chest. "You want to lose money, I can make that happen."

He winks at me, which is bold for him. I like that bold Axel is back even if his confidence is currently built off the fact he thinks he's a luckless loser. He turns his sculpted torso back to the machine, reaches up, and cranks the lever old school, even though you can now just hit a button on the machine instead. The machine spins and flashes and makes a bunch of annoying noises.

Four Leaf Clover. Seven. Top Hat.

Not a winner.

He pulls the handle again.

Another non-winning combination.

Again.

Same thing.

He looks up at me with the biggest 'I told you so' look on his face. Billy is standing behind Frankie, but watching us. He points. "See? Statistics don't lie, people. We're all losers here."

"You're a World Champion two times over," I remind him. "What's the English expression I'm looking for... Shut the fuck up."

Everyone crows with laughter, including Axel. I squeeze his shoulder and lean down, whispering in his ear. "Just so you know, even if you aren't lucky here, I can guarantee you'll be lucky later. If you want."

A visible shiver ripples down his spine and his hand jerks as my lips ghost his neck. He pulls the lever inadvertently.

Four Leaf Clover. Four Leaf Clover. Four Leaf Clover.

The machine erupts in bells and whistles, sirens and lights. The total on the counter starts spinning and ends at $5,000.

"Axel Walsh just beat the odds," Billy hollers as he laughs.

"Guess I'm your lucky charm, just like you're mine," I tell him.

He turns three shades of pink before covering his face with his hands and laughing into them while everyone around him jumps and cheers.

I'm so damn hot my shirt is sticking to me but if you think I'm leaving this dance floor you are dead fucking wrong. Because I'm chest-to-chest with Gabriel and his hips are bumping mine as his arms are draped lazily over my shoulders and it's the closest to heaven I'll probably ever be.

"You are *hard*," I whisper-shout into his ear.

"Because you are *gorgeous*." He pushes his hips against mine again and I feel his length, solid and thick against my pelvis.

After my big win, we cashed out and Lucia and Frankie insisted we go dancing. So now here we are, two and a half hours after midnight, in the middle of a packed dance floor at a club in the bowels of an off-strip hotel. I'm drunk and horny and, for the first time in way too long, happy. And it has nothing to do with the five grand in my pocket either.

"You are the one who looks like a model right now," I tell him and yank him even closer with my arm that's wrapped around his waist. "You're hotter than a crocodile sunning himself on the equator."

Gabriel laughs, tipping his head back and exposing that

long, thick neck of his. My mouth waters at the sight. I bet it tastes salty and delicious and if I nuzzle him there he'll still smell like that aftershave he wears which is dark and sensuous like leather and sandalwood. I do it without even thinking. Nuzzle him and let my tongue slip out and taste his skin. My thoughts were spot on and, oh God, I could come from it.

He digs the long, strong fingers of his left hand into my hair, gripping it and pulling my head back. It's a little rough and a total turn-on. "You keep that up Axel, and I am fucking you tonight."

"Is that a promise or a threat?"

I'm playing with fire. And my feelings are a puddle of gasoline. If they ignite, this will end badly. I am *not* supposed to have feelings here.

"It's both," Gabriel replies, leaning in so close our lips are almost touching. "I want you, Axel. So much I can barely breathe."

And that's it. Those words and the soft yearning look in his midnight blue eyes are the match that ignites my feelings. The stupid things that have gotten me into nothing but trouble every time I give in to them. "I want you too. More than I can stand."

He's holding my head now, between his hands, and our lips brush but then suddenly there's another hand gripping my shoulder from behind and pulling me backward. It's my best friend. Or should I say former best friend because the title should definitely be stripped from Billy for interrupting this moment. "We're heading home, and I think you two should too. Before you're bounced from the club for having sex in public."

"We weren't having sex," Gabriel replies. "Yet."

Billy chuckles. "Let's go, French Romeo."

Billy shoves me toward the exit and I oblige, reaching back to lace my fingers with Gabriel's. The girls and Nick are in front of us and after a few stairs and a maze of hallways we're out on the street. A giant SUV is waiting there with Frankie's body-guard Jack in front of it. The club in a casino off the strip was the only way Frankie could convince her bodyguard to wait in the car, because the 'threat' was lessened at these less popular locations, and Nick, a former bodyguard and probably a former MI6 spy or something, was with them.

At this point, almost everything on the street is closed and even the street lights above seem dimmer. But there is one pink and gold neon sign still flashing brightly directly across the street from the place we just left. It catches Lucia's eye and she stumbles toward it. Nick scoops her around the waist and stops her from walking straight out into the street. *"Attention, chouette."*

"Is that French?" I ask because Nick is a Brit.

"Oui," Gabriel answers.

"I need to learn a second language if I'm going to fit in," I mutter. "How many do you speak?"

"Fluently?" Gabe asks, and I nod. "French, English, Italian, and Spanish. I am decent in German and Japanese. I can ask for the bathroom or a beer or a condom in Cantonese."

"What else do you need?" I quip.

He laughs but our attention moves back to Lucia who is trying to free herself from Nick, but he doesn't let her go. "Put me down! Let's sneak in and see who gets married at two-thirty in the morning."

He laughs but she wiggles harder and manages to break free and make a run for it. Frankie jogs across the street after her. Billy chases them both. Nick and Jack both swear and shake their heads. I tug on Gabriel's hand. "I guess we're crashing a wedding."

Lucia has the tacky chapel door open and is slipping inside by the time I'm dragging Gabe up the rickety white steps. The interior lobby of this place looks like someone took the set of the

Brady Bunch and every rhinestone on every jumpsuit Elvis ever owned, put it all in a blender and then threw it all over this room.

The carpet is deep green shag. The walls are wood paneled but they're covered in bejeweled velvet paintings. A cat with emerald stone eyes in a wedding veil marrying a Doberman with onyx eyes and a ruby studded collar. A flamingo in pink velvet with a diamond-encrusted tiara marrying a seagull in a bowtie made out of purple glimmering stones. Lucia has already advanced past all that visual chaos to the heavy wood doors in front.

A tired-looking older man in a very cheap suit behind a veneer desk that makes Ikea furniture look expensive asks if he can be of assistance. "I don't think so, my girlfriend just wants to crash a wedding," Nick explains.

"Oh there isn't a wedding happening at the moment," the man replies, standing up and shuffling out from behind his desk.

Lucia's entire face drops in an almost comical fashion. "Nick, we're going to have to get married."

"What?" Frankie gasps.

Lucia just shrugs. "I want to see a wedding. Vegas without a wedding isn't really Vegas, is it?"

"Honey, I will marry you in a heartbeat, and you know it," Nick says calmly like this isn't the most absurd thing he's ever heard. It's definitely the craziest thing I've heard.

"I hate to use the one sober brain cell I have left at the moment," Frankie interjects, and she's kind of wobbling so Billy steps up behind her and holds her shoulders. "But Dad will be devastated if you get married without him."

"Call him," Lucia suggests.

"Nope," Frankie replies. "He's in England, remember?"

"Well someone has to get married," Lucia whines. "It will be *so* romantic."

"We have commitment ceremonies too," the man from the desk explains. "No paperwork required but all the romance."

"We'll take one of those!" Lucia announces.

I laugh. This girl is a hoot. Maybe a little nuts, but definitely a hoot. Frankie's pretty face scrunches up. "I think I can allow that. If it's not legally binding. But Dad might still murder us."

"Or I can do it," Gabriel announces.

"You can get married?" Billy asks and when he nods every single set of eyes in the place, even the stranger from the desk, turns to me.

"What? Who? Me? Us?" I question, startled by this turn of events.

"Well, I can't marry Billy or Nick and I don't think I'm Jack's type," Gabriel says and Frankie's bodyguard nods.

"Affirmative," Jack says flatly. "I'm a boob man and you don't have those."

"No. I do not," Gabriel replies and turns to me. "Wanna fake marry me? That'll definitely make headlines."

"Yeah it will, but..."

"Oh come on!" Lucia whines. "Just do the commitment thing! For fun! I'll pay! I got a hundred bucks!"

"That will get you a commitment ceremony with the flower package," the old man informs her.

Lucia claps once—loudly. "Sold!"

"Oh my God, this is out of control," I exclaim and now adrenaline is floating through my veins, surfing on the booze already clogging them. My eyes lock with Gabriel's. "Are you serious?"

"No, but yes. I mean, what the hell, right?" Gabriel says. "It's harmless."

Billy clasps my shoulder again. "I can fake marry Frankie instead. Her dad won't kill me. He needs me to win races."

I smile. "Nah. I mean, I'll do it. If they'll even do it with two mates. I know it's not exactly welcome in a lot of States."

"Nevada allows same-sex marriages and commitment cere-monies," the man pipes in and points to a painting in the corner, by an exit sign, that I missed. It's fat Elvis dipping skinny Elvis in front of the chapel and kissing.

"Okay fuck it. Let's pretend," I say, and Lucia jumps up and hoots and then falls over.

Ten minutes later, I'm at the end of the aisle, holding a fucking bouquet of gardenias, and Gabriel is at the front of this god-awfully decorated church that smells like moth balls. Billy is at my side walking me down the aisle to a song called "Peace" by Taylor Swift, that Frankie insisted on. The lyrics are achingly speak of a secret love that may or may not be doomed. *Touché.*

Nick is standing up as Gabe's best man. Lucia is weaving her drunk way down the aisle tossing hot pink rose petals, like a hot mess of a flower girl, and Frankie is filming the whole damn thing on her phone.

I get to the front and lock eyes with Gabe and we both burst out laughing. I miss most of what the 'minister' (the same guy from the cheap desk, only now he's in a polyester priest outfit) says but I think I hear the words love and commitment and soul mates.

I have tears brimming in my eyes when he tells me to repeat after him. The tears are pure hysteria at the absurdity of this situation. Gabriel borrowed a jacket from the church wardrobe, but I refused. So I'm still in my sweaty shirt and he's wearing a green and red plaid blazer. It's like Santa's dinner jacket. I'm marrying fucking Vegas Santa. And I'm sure the laughter Gabriel is trying to stifle is because Frankie attached a veil to the back of my head with a clip that's sure to rip out what little hair it's clipped to.

"I, Axel, promise to spend my life…"

"I, Axel, promise to spend my life…" I repeat, my voice wobbly and weak from booze and laughter.

"Filling our moments together with love and laughter."

"Filling our moments together with love and laughter."

"You're off to a good start, *mon amour*," Gabriel interrupts and giggles.

Billy snickers beside me. I elbow him.

"I, Gabriel, promise to spend my life…" the minister leads.

"I, Gabriel, promise to spend my life filling our moments with love and laughter, some epic orgasms, and whatever the hell else you want," Gabriel says, and I'm not even surprised he's going off-script. "Because you have made my life infinitely better in a ridiculously short time, Axel Jericho Maximus Walsh Hemming and I vow to do the same to you. Even if it means peeling back all your tightly folded, neatly pressed, emotional layers, one by one. I'll do it because it'll be worth it. *You* are worth it."

Oh shit.

I think the reason for the tears in my eyes has changed.

"Well now… I don't have that written down. Let me find my place…" the fake minister murmurs.

"Can I just kiss him already?" I ask.

"Yes. Fine, we can—"

I grab Gabriel's face in my hands and pull him into the most searing, scorching, passionate kiss I have ever given anyone. And I mean every single heart-melting moment of it.

It's all fun and games until we get back to the hotel and we're alone in front of our room doors. Jesus Christ I just fake married my fake boyfriend and nothing has ever felt so real in my whole damn life.

I rub the back of my neck as we stand face-to-face. "I don't suppose you want to come in and, maybe, consummate this fake marriage with some real sex?"

I flash him a grin that's all brash and undaunted but inside I'm kind of dying. Nothing about my feelings are fake anymore and I'm trying not to freak out. I've never had feelings this strong for anyone. Luckily I think Axel is still too drunk to see my truth or read me like a book because he turns that shade of pink I love to see on his cheeks and grabs the collar of the utterly tacky jacket I forgot to give back, and whispers, "I think of all the bad ideas we've had tonight, that is the best one."

"So... *oui?*"

"*Oui.* I would like to consummate this," Axel replies, his mouth already touching mine. "Preferably with your dick in my ass but I'm also not opposed to mine in yours."

"*Merde,*" I whisper, light-headed because all the blood in

my body just started racing toward my cock. "Fake married Axel is a blunt, dirty little thing and I am here for it."

I pull my key card out of my pants and tap it on the hotel room door. As we tumble inside, Axel says, "There's nothing little about me."

I think of the other night with my lips around his cock. "I think I remember that, but let's get naked and you can remind me."

And we spend the next several minutes doing just that. Our clothes fall away as we kiss and make our way to the bed. The only thing we both leave on are the tin rings that were included in the package that Lucia bought. We fall together onto the bed, I'm under him on top of the ample pile of plush pillows and the downy comforter and I close my eyes and revel in the feel of all his warm, bare flesh against all of mine.

He kisses my neck and rolls his hips, our cocks pressing and rubbing against each other. I groan in a way that sounds both feral and anguished. "Don't make me come before the big show, husband."

He kind of freezes for half a second, but I feel it and my eyes open. His face is so close it's blurry but I see the flicker of sobriety that passes across his angular features. "Call me that again."

I flip us, so he's on the bottom. "Husband."

"Fuck..." Axel pants. "Why is that hot?'

"I don't know but it is," I admit before I kiss him slowly.

Minutes tick by as we explore each other's bodies with our tongues, teeth, and hands. More than once I have to beg him to stop to keep from coming and he does the same to me, especially when I'm sucking on the head of his perfect, cut dick and pressing two fingers into him.

His hips twist and he grabs my wrist with both hands. "Stop. I want you. Not just your fingers."

"I'm warming you up, *mon amour*," I remind him. As if to provide an example I push my fingers in as far as they will go, to the knuckle, and scissor them a little. He winces and then groans, the first in pain and the second in pleasure. But his grip on my wrist gets tighter still.

"I am warmer than your racing engine, Gabe," he promises and his lips find my earlobe where he proceeds to suck it into his hot little mouth and then nip it with his perfect teeth. "Do you have condoms?"

"Yeah."

"Put one on."

I hate that I have to roll away from him to grab them out of my night table drawer but I do. I am so glad I made the impetuous, hopeful decision to buy them on the way home from the track today. I hadn't been traveling with any since the accusations because I was *not* about to have sex with anyone. My trust issues run that deep. But after our encounter the other night... I started to hope.

I roll the condom on and grab the bottle of lube off my nightstand. I look down at him, all flushed skin and eager eyes and swollen lips and I feel my first *coup de foudre*. It's a French term that means 'strike of lightning' and it's how we describe love. The real, sudden passionate kind. Like love at first sight.

"Are you okay?" Axel asks, pulling himself up to his elbows.

"Yeah, I just..." *fell in love at first sight, even though I've seen you a hundred times before.* "Was wondering how you want to do this."

His dark eyebrows shoot up. "You've never...?"

"No. I know *how* to do this." I smile and a soundless laugh pushes out from my chest. "I just mean there are options, stylistically. What's your preference?"

"Stylistically?" Axel grins. "My husband is truly the son of a fashion king, talking style while I'm naked and leaking and begging for his cock."

I grin so hard I think I tear a facial muscle or two. "Say it again."

"Husband."

I grab his waist and yank him to the edge of the bed with a strength I didn't even know I had. Axel is taller than me and his frame bulkier. I shouldn't be able to move him without a bit of a struggle, but I do. "Feet on the ground. Stomach on the mattress. Now. *Husband.*"

I can barely pronounce the H in that fucking word, or any word. Curse of the French accent, but he still seems turned on by it because he lets out a gasping breath and does exactly as I demanded, even arching his back a little so he's presenting his perfect ass to me.

My cock is vibrating with desire now. I finger him again, with lube, but we're both impatient, and in seconds I'm pushing the head of my cock past his first ring of muscle. Everything changes. The mood gets heavier, the air in the room seems hotter, the noises Axel starts making are deeper, and the feelings I'm ignoring in my heart get stronger.

Sex is intimacy, always, even when it's just fun and games. I've always known that. There's a level of trust and respect that I've always had for all my partners, even the ones whose last names I can't remember or never knew. But this... this with Axel is more than that. It's more than I've ever known.

I admit that to myself as my cock sinks deeper and deeper until my pubic bone pushes into the rounds of his perfect ass. I stay that way, unmoving, giving him time to adjust to my size and my heart time to absorb the size of these feelings. Oh my God, I might be falling in love.

I bite my bottom lip to keep from saying it out loud. Or anything. Now is not the time for words. Axel grunts and clenches and it's his green flag. His way of telling me to go. So I do. Moving in and out of him with a rhythm that comes easily. I slide a palm up the center of his back, feeling every vertebra as I glide to his neck. He reaches up and circles my wrist with his long fingers, pulling me forward as I thrust. Pressing his lips to my palm and then biting down on it as the movement changes my angle inside him. I must have found his sweet spot. He shudders.

"Faster, Gabe. Please. Faster," he pants.

I grab his hip with my free hand and flick my hips harder and faster. My balls are so tight and straining for release but he has to go first. Anything less would be a failure. He groans so deep I swear the walls shake. And when he lets go of my hand I snake it under us to wrap it around his dick. I keep my rhythm hard and fast and match it with my hand's motion around his cock. I'm rewarded with his warm, sticky release coating my fingers, and the duvet, seconds later. I'm not coherent enough to really enjoy it though because my own orgasm rips through me almost immediately.

I wail and collapse onto his back, biting his shoulder to keep the sound muffled. He drops forward, flat on the mattress, taking my body with him. I roll to the side and we lie there, me face up and Axel face down, both gasping for breath.

Eventually, we're both sucking air into our lungs in even, steady breaths. I am exhausted and I wonder if he's already passed out when he slides his hand across the small space between us and covers my own with it. His fingers curl between mine and I rub the side of his pinky with my thumb.

I pull the condom off with my free hand and drop it to the ground. The last thing I remember is a soft tink sound as our cheap wedding bands knock together on our intertwined hands.

MY HEAD IS ABSOLUTELY POUNDING.

Oh no. Wait. That's the hotel room door.

I groan. It echoes.

Oh no. Wait. That's someone groaning beside me.

Gabriel.

The pounding gets louder. I open my eyes and I swear to god it *hurts*. "Can you sprain your eyelids drinking?"

I hear a soft, but rough chuckle beside me and then a hand on the small of my bare back. Right. I'm naked. With a dull, but satisfying ache between my butt cheeks.

The entire night comes flooding back to me. Every magical, maniacal, extremely stupid moment. Now my eyes are wide, unblinking, focused on Gabriel. He's got one forearm thrown across his forehead. His eyes are still shut. He's naked and sporting wood. Beautiful wood. I give my head an actual shake as I start to sit up and instantly regret both decisions.

I groan again.

The pounding on the door gets harder. More urgent. Gabriel's eyes flutter open. "Who the fuck is trying to break the sound barrier and the door?"

"I have no idea," I reply, my voice raspy, my heart thumping at the memories. Does he remember everything?

His eyes land on mine. He smiles. "Morning, husband."

Oh my God. He remembers.

"Gabriel!"

It's his father.

Oh fuck. It's his father!

I leap out of bed, my feet tangle in my pants on the floor, and I tip over, my shoulder clipping the night table. I curse and bite back a yelp. Gabriel is up, and in front of me, blurry-eyed. "Are you alright?"

"Answer the door before he breaks it down," I whisper, sitting up and rubbing my shoulder. "I'll hide in the shower."

"It's all glass."

"The closet."

"A little too on-point, don't you think?" Gabriel counters. "And why? We're supposed to be dating. You being in here isn't scandalous."

"But I said this would be professional," I argue and stand up, grabbing my pants.

There's more pounding on the door.

Gabriel lets out a typical Parisienne 'pft' sound and he reaches out to help me up. *"J'arrive! Attendez une minute, Papa!"* Gabriel yells in French and I know enough to know he's telling his dad to hold on a minute.

We rush around the apartment, grabbing clothes and throwing ourselves into them. I end up in his shirt, and he's in mine, which is inside out. I only have one sock. He's barefoot as he runs a hand through his hair and reaches for the door. I am already the color of a fire engine when Louis walks in, followed by Damien.

Both do a stutter-step as they see me leaning casually against the door frame to the bedroom part of the suite. I have my arms crossed, bruised shoulder against the door frame, and legs crossed, sockless foot over socked one. I must look like a fucking lunatic.

"Axel," Louis says my name pointedly and the hairs on the back of my neck stand up.

"He decided to swing by early, so we could talk about strategy," Gabriel lies so easily I almost believe him. "You know, where we'll pop up together next."

"I suppose that would be your honeymoon," Damien says, pulling his phone out of his suit pocket and tapping it a couple times before holding it up, screen out.

There, in big bold print, is a list of Google search results for Gabriel Allard. And every single headline includes the word "Married" and my name. I stop breathing. I mean, literally. My lungs have been dipped in quick-dry cement. Gabriel leans in, eyes narrowed, and then he plucks the phone from Damien and taps one of the links. It's Perez Hilton's site and a video at the top of the article instantly starts playing. It's Gabe and me at the altar, making out and laughing and being cheered on wildly by everyone.

"Oh, yeah," Gabriel nods. "About that..."

"You got *married?*" Louis is talking to me, not his son. In fact, he sidesteps Gabriel to stand in front of me. I'm taller than him, by a lot, but I feel much smaller right now.

"No. Not technically... sir." Did I just 'sir' him? Yesterday I was calling him Louis. Now he's sir? I gulp. "It was a commitment ceremony."

"It looks like a wedding but with no legal documents," Gabriel explains.

"Oh my fucking God," Damien hisses. He turns to me, pointing a chubby finger at my face. "You're fired."

Oh shit.

Gabriel steps between Damien's hand and my face. "No! He's not. And fuck you, you're fired."

"Nobody is fired!" Louis bellows and turns away from me. He runs his hands through his silvery hair as he paces in front of the oval coffee table, whispering to himself in French.

I've righted myself, giving up on the uncasual lean in the doorway, and watch Louis, every muscle in my body tight like an overturned piano. Gabriel steps away from Damien and moves to stand next to me in the doorway, taking my hand in his own. He laces his fingers through mine and I feel slightly better. It gives me the courage to speak.

"Look, I know that the confusion around this isn't ideal. It's another mess to explain away," I start and pause to clear my throat as Louis stops pacing and stands ramrod straight, hands clenching the lapels of his blazer while he glares at me. "It looks spontaneous and irrational, but if it also looks authentic, people won't mind. If we don't call it off or backtrack, the public will cheer for it, just like Billy and the others did."

"And is it? Authentic?" Louis demands, his eyes now on his son. He's searching his face for visual confirmation, not just the words Gabe's about to say.

"Yes. Sort of," Gabriel replies, shocking me. "I mean, it could, maybe, be real if it didn't have to be fake."

"Well it has to be fake," Damien points out and glares at me. "You agreed to fake. You signed an NDA. Your career—"

"I'm not going to do anything that makes Gabe look bad," I announce and feel my cheeks heat when I look at his father and see his hazel eyes are focused on the carpet in the bedroom. Because I think the condom from last night is still lying there.

Gabriel glances over his shoulder and then reaches back and pulls the door to the bedroom closed. "Listen, both of you, nothing has changed. This isn't a catastrophe. If anything, it gives everyone more reason to stop talking about the woman's accusation."

"False accusation," I add, and Gabriel gives me a soft, grateful smile.

"Yeah but you two getting divorced in a couple weeks is going to create a new scandal," Damien barks, and he's glaring at me again.

I realize, with a cold, sobering clarity that it's only my career that's going to get fucked by this. My life. Again. Because of a guy. If this ends. I mean *when...* right? Because it has to. Doesn't it?

"Okay. It's done," Louis says quietly and he starts to pace again. This time, when he shoots me a quick glance, it's not nearly as menacing as it was. In fact, it's kind of... normal. "So now we move on. They'll ask you about it, Gabriel. A lot. And Axel, they're going to want to know more about you. We'll have to set up an interview or something with you."

"I'm never the guy in front of a camera or microphone," I remind him.

Louis smiles. "That changed when you had a midnight commitment ceremony with my son."

"It was more like three a.m.," Gabriel clarifies and smiles coyly as he gets nothing but glares from all of us.

Fuck. The idea of being interviewed makes my skin crawl. Louis is on a roll and he continues barking out ideas as he paces. "Gabe, that ring never leaves your finger. I know there's no jewelry during races but put up a fuss about it, like you don't want to take it off. I'll pay a fine if I have to. People will swoon over your sentimentality. What is that thing made out of, anyway? Tin foil?"

"I think maybe aluminum?"

"It's definitely going to turn my finger green," I say and shrug because honestly, it could make my finger fall off and I wouldn't care.

"I'll get my assistant to look into new rings. Nothing flashy or expensive," Louis says. "Oh, I wish I had a jewelry line."

"It's definitely an area to look into," I say and Damien tries to melt me into the carpet with his beady eyes.

Gabriel presses a fleeting hand to my back and then moves toward the door. "I have to be at the track in an hour. Can you guys go so I can get ready? We'll talk about this more after qualifying and press."

"But—" Damien starts.

"Yes. We will see you there," Louis says, cutting off the disgruntled employee and gently pushing him to the open door.

I glance around the room but can't see the other sock so I decide I'm just going to have to do the walk of shame without it. But when I pick up my shoes and start toward the door, Gabe reaches out and grabs me by the bicep, rooting me in place. The door closes behind Damien and Louis, leaving us alone again.

His gaze heats. "You don't have to go. Unless you want to."

"I don't want to, but you need to get ready, right?"

He smiles and moves my hand toward the front of his pants. "First I need help with this." He presses my palm into his hard cock. "Have you ever tried to drive over two-hundred kilometers an hour with a rock-hard cock? It's nearly impossible."

I laugh and he reaches up and kisses my neck before growling into it. "Wanna take a shower with your husband?"

"Yeah. I do."

THERE IS no way to deny the change. I was able to walk around the race tracks before without much more than a few curious glances. Now, I'm being flat-out stared at. No one is even pretending not to notice me. It's creating a ball of anxiety in the middle of my gut. And the phone buzzing repeatedly in my pocket isn't helping.

It's my sister. Mostly. She's messaged me nine times and called me twenty-four times. I have yet to answer, or even look at the texts. There's also a few hundred—yes, hundred—emails from news outlets, reporters, and even the freaking docuseries crew that follows the drivers around. They have never, in the history of ever, interviewed a wife or girlfriend of a driver before. Technically, they have interviewed a boyfriend, but only because two drivers are dating. Cristian Rivera and Jasper Nord. Oh, and I think they interviewed Ben Carpenter but he's an engineer and so even though he's dating a driver, it's different. I'm nothing. No one. And I'm *not* calling them back.

I watch Gabriel suit up from my now favorite corner of the garage. The ring on my finger feels like a neon billboard, I swear to God there isn't a set of eyes in the place that hasn't stared at it for at least a few seconds since I got here. I keep twisting it around my ring finger with my thumb. The movement gives me comfort, especially when I catch Gabriel doing it too. Until Bob Johnson comes over and has what turns into a heated, heavily whispered debate with him. By the time it's done, Bob is sweating more than normal, his face flushed as he stomps over to his seat on the pit wall. Gabriel shoves his hands in his gloves and looks over at me before pulling on his helmet. The ring didn't come off.

I wonder about the fallout from that. I know drivers aren't allowed to wear jewelry. It's been deemed a safety hazard. Billy once explained to me it's the only reason he doesn't have a Prince Albert. A piece of info I did not need to know about my bestie.

Anyway, now I spend the entire qualifying worrying about whether that ring is going to burn through Gabriel's finger if he crashes or something on his car catches fire. And then I stop worrying about the ring and just worry about everything else. This is a dangerous sport. He could be seriously hurt or killed at any moment. I can't believe Louis lets his son do this. I can't believe Gabriel wants to risk his life weekly. Sure I've worried about Billy on-and-off through the years and I've watched him have some crashes, but he's always walked away. And even when they happened it didn't feel as sickening as thinking about it happening to Gabriel. Am I the worst best friend ever?

I didn't intend to fake marry, or fake commit, or whatever, to Gabriel, but now that the world thinks I did it, I don't want to have to fake mourn him either. Only it wouldn't actually be fake. Because my feelings for him are real. I start to pace in my little corner of the garage, my fists balled up by my sides. Gabriel makes it through the first round of qualifying, finishing eleventh, and then he ups his game and finishes the Q2 in ninth.

Both very solid and respectable. In Q1 he finishes in fifth. Fucking fifth!

I breathe a sigh of relief followed by a hoot of victory, and one of the mechanics high-fives me. Another slaps me on the back and Louis hugs me tightly. "I like who he is becoming," Louis whispers in my ear.

I just nod, not knowing what the hell to say to that. And now Gabriel's rushing through the garage and he's making his way to me— uninterrupted. Only one mechanic, the same guy who high-fived me, but other than that, no Mayflower staffer is congratulating him. No one is celebrating. I realize the garage is fairly empty.

"Where is everyone?" I ask.

"Sterling is P1 so they're off to watch his interview and congratulate him over by the pit lane," Gabriel says, smiling as he yanks off his fire retardant balaclava and his sandy hair sticks up every which way.

I step closer and smooth down the left side, then the right. It's not for him and his interviews, it's because I love the feel of his hair in my hands. "All of them?"

"As Luke says in *Star Wars*, he's their only hope," Gabriel replies calmly. In fact, he's so resigned to the fact that I'm bothered by how unbothered he is.

"First of all, Luke didn't say it," I inform him and I sound unreasonably annoyed at his misquote, I know. Really, it's the way this team ignores Gabriel that annoys me. "Princess Leia Organa says it about Obi-Wan Kenobi. In a hologram message."

Gabriel's eyes dance with bottled-up laughter. "I didn't realize I committed to a *Star Wars* nerd."

"You didn't. It's basic common knowledge," I say and shake my head. "Whatever. It's also irrelevant. This is a big deal, you're fucking fifth. More than just that guy should be here to congratulate you."

"That guy is Adam," Gabriel explains and Adam waves when he hears his name. "He's the lead mechanic on my car so he doesn't have a choice. And the humbling truth of my seat here at Mayflower is that they only gave it to me because my father invested. No one expects me to win and no one is going to bother patting me on the back. If they could get rid of me, they would."

"But you're doing well," I argue as we walk out of the garage together. He's sucking on a water bottle and I'm really glad the sun has dipped low in the horizon, behind the towering buildings of the strip, because if I could clearly see his full mouth wrap around that bottle I would get hard. "I've watched rookie drivers go a whole season without placing in the top ten. You almost scored points."

"Almost is didn't. They're the same thing," Gabriel says. He stops just short of the press tent. All the other drivers are already there. His dad stayed back in the garage so it's just the two of us. "I appreciate your indignant wife routine here, and that you've got my back, but I knew what I was signing up for when I got my seat this way. The thing with the assistant, and the paternity suit earlier, none of that helped. But I wasn't going to be respected even if those things hadn't happened. It's fine. I am not crying myself to sleep at night. You can stay over tonight and make sure."

He winks at me before walking off to do his interviews.

I sigh and watch him go and then make my way back to the parking lot. I'll meet him at the hotel. My phone buzzes again and I whip it out. The name Cordy illuminates my screen.

"Do not freak out," I say flatly instead of hello.

"You are fucking married?" Cordelia screeches so loudly that I think she may have perforated my eardrum. I immediately move the phone a few inches from my ear. "Married! To your boss's son? What the ever-loving hell Axel Hemming!"

"Okay well, don't believe everything you read," I tell her, holding the phone with just the microphone by my mouth so if she starts yelling again my eardrums aren't in danger.

What's left of the sun has streaked the sky gold and pink, and the warm, acrid air swirls around me with hints of oil and gasoline and burned rubber. It's not actually all that unpleasant. It feels a bit like home because it reminds me of Gabe. I touch my thumb to the band again and interrupt Cordy as she calls me every synonym for stupid that she can think of.

"Relax, okay? Will you just shut up and listen to me?" I bark and she finally gets silent. "I didn't marry him. We were drunk and we had a commitment ceremony. It was a lark. And funny. And not that big a deal."

"So why are there photos of you all over Instagram at the Qualifying wearing a fucking wedding band, Axe?" Cordy demands. "And why is an F1 blog reporting that Gabriel is going to be fined for not taking off his wedding ring before going out in the car?"

"How much is the fine?" I ask.

"Why? You gonna pay it for him?" Cordy snaps. "This guy going to swindle you too, like the last one?"

Ouch. Well, that was definitely below the belt.

I stop walking. The pavement under my feet is so warm it feels sticky. I can see waves of heat rising up all over the parking lot. I want nothing more than to be in an air-conditioned hotel room, lying naked on the bed, waiting for Gabe, but I'm also kind of sick of my sister's judgment. "You know what, Cordy, that was a fucking asshole thing to say."

She huffs out a frustrated breath and it takes her a minute but she finally says something. "I'm sorry, okay? I just... I worry about you. You let that asshole Eric take more from you than he ever gave you. I never understood why. And I just... I mean, I want you to get back on your feet. I'm trying to help you by selling your loft. And in my humble opinion, you need to take a break from dating after the train wreck that was half a decade with Eric. Not marry your billionaire boss's son. Does Louis Allard know?"

"Yes."

"How is this going to affect your career trajectory?" she demands. "I mean, if you hurt Gabriel, Louis will fire you. I guarantee it. The world knows he lives for his kid. And if Gabriel gets bored of you... he can have you fired. Daddy does whatever he wants."

"It's not as bad as it seems," I reply because looking back over what I've seen with Gabriel and Louis, yeah, it's sort of how Cordy sees it. But there's more to it. There's an actual respect and partnership between the father and son. Louis is more like Gabriel's manager. And I don't think he would pick his own dad to be so up in his business but he wants to be the good son. "And you know, this thing with Gabriel... Louis is on board. Will he always be? Probably not. But I also have seen enough of both him and Gabriel to know that they'll handle whatever happens next with professionalism and respect."

"What are you not telling me, big brother?" Cordy asks sharply.

"Can you just trust me?"

"I trust you. I don't trust your judgment though."

Another punch, this time to my ego. Nice sis. "You've made mistakes too, Cordy. Remember that kid who worked at the surf shop? The one who played you all summer long until you brought him to the family barbeque and he spontaneously started auditioning for Dad over the potato salad? Or what about your date for the Oscars that one year. The one who wanted to shag Mom?"

"Oh fuck, Axe," she snaps. "First of all Cordy dated those losers, and this is Delia you're talking to."

"Must be nice to have a split personality."

"Ha!" she barks out loudly. "And second of all, Axel, I dumped both those idiots on the spot. Erased their numbers, blocked them on socials, and I would have burned their houses to the ground if someone had given me a match. You, on the other hand, took Eric back every single time he did something to hurt or gaslight you. Every fucking time for six years. So I am very sorry if I'm worried about this new boyfriend-slash-commitment ceremony partner. I'm not convinced you've learned from your mistakes."

"I have."

She sighs. "Gabe Allard was accused of fathering a kid earlier this year."

"And a test proved he wasn't the father."

"But now he's being accused of groping a woman," she argues. "But he runs off to marry you? How long have you even been dating?"

I've reached the end of my rope. "Anything else? Do you want to remind me how badly I did in the seventh-grade play? Or perhaps we can rehash that time I tripped at one of Dad's movie premieres when I was fourteen and knocked over two photographers. Would you like to rub my nose in that mistake?"

"Axel..." Her tone is contrite, but I don't care.

"Is the condo sale finalized yet?"

"Should have final papers tomorrow," she says.

"Good. Please don't call me when you get them. Just email them," I reply and press end on the call.

It stings. But deep down, I know my sister might be right. I mean, have I really grown? I was worried about Gabriel when I found out who he was after that first kiss years ago. It's one of the reasons I didn't try to pursue him. He felt so much bigger than me. Like he was Prince Charming and I was Cinderella, only the shoe would never fit. And has anything really changed?

He's still everything I'm not—worldly, confident, passionate, and easily bored. And I'm pretty fucking boring.

Yeah, this rollercoaster we're on is fun, but fun can be fleeting. Even if I wanted to stick around after this job is done, and his name is cleared, would he want me to? Or will he be bored of me? Is what makes this so fun for Gabe the fact that it's make-believe?

Those thoughts stew in my brain the whole way to the hotel.

"*N*E T'INQUIÈTE PAS. *Ne t'inquiète pas. Ne t'inquiète pas.*" I repeat 'don't worry' in French to myself all the time when I'm stressed about something. To be honest, I haven't been stressed in a long while. Not stressed enough to chant to myself. But I can't get Axel's face out of my head.

When Axel talked about the way the team wasn't supporting me, the look on his face was so... concerned. He was truly baffled. I hated every excruciating moment of trying to explain to him the simple truth of this. It was embarrassing, and the humiliation of it all has settled over me like a sheen of sweat after a particularly long and hot race.

And then that dick of a reporter Nico Hilliard made it worse when he asked me about Axel. "I hear congratulations are in order. Not just for a solid top ten position for the race tomorrow, but because it's your first as a married man."

"Thanks. Yeah. Well, it was technically a commitment ceremony," I clarify and smile, trying to focus on memories of last night with Axel and not this dickhead's smug face. He's smiling like he's got a knife up his jacket sleeve he's waiting to shiv me with though, so it's hard to ignore him. "If I got married without my dad, there would be hell to pay."

"Of course." Nico's mean-hearted smile deepens. "You don't do much without your dad. And besides, who would pay for it? You know, your boyfriend just lost his company. And he's selling his house."

Is he seriously trying to say Axel might be a gold digger? I fight to keep my face from showing anger because the idea makes me furious. Instead, I roll my eyes. "I don't discuss my hus...partner's personal life. Thanks for the well wishes. Do you want my thoughts on how I'll do in the race tomorrow since I'm starting fifth?"

"Sure. Tell us what you think," Nico says all too adamantly. It reeks of sarcasm. "I asked Bob when he did his interview but he didn't have much to say about the team's strategy for you tomorrow. Is there one?"

"Depends on the weather, but if it's hot and dry like today then tire management will be my focus," I mutter and then thank him for his time with the biggest, fakest smile on my face before moving on, my fists balled angrily at my sides.

Now back at the hotel, I take a deep breath as I step off the elevator and exhale slowly as I proceed down the empty hall. I get to my door, lean my head against it for a second, trying to push down all those uncomfortable feelings that have been swirling and tap my key card. The light flicks to green and I push the handle down.

The suite smells wonderful in a bunch of different ways. I smell savory food and some lavender and melting wax. But I don't smell the simple crisp scent of Axel's cologne. And I don't see him anywhere. "Axel?"

There's no response as I walk slowly into the room. By the couch is a room service tray with silver domes on it and a pitcher of mint ice water. Candles flicker from the bar and the coffee table, which are the only lights in the room. I stick my head in the bedroom and the place is empty, bed pristinely made and a small cluster of fresh lavender is on the night table in a very small, ornate crystal vase.

In the bathroom on the counter, propped up on my toiletry kit, between the black marble double sinks, is a note on hotel stationery. Axel's handwriting is much like him—neat and precise.

Gabe,

I know that you need to focus tonight. I ordered you some food and will be next door if you need anything. Fresh lavender always calms me down. Not an easy thing to find in Vegas, but it was worth it if it helps you.

See you at the paddock tomorrow.

Your husband, ;)

Axe

I re-read the note about ten times. I don't know how I feel about it. I mean, it's logical. I have never spent the night before a race with anyone other than my trainer or strategist. Back in F2, when people believed I earned my spot, I would sometimes hang out with the other drivers. We'd play a couple video games, but everyone was back in their own rooms by nine.

The note is sweet and the food and lavender means he went out of his way for me. Still, I don't like that he's not here. I spend forty-five minutes telling myself it's for the best as I shower and pick my way through the chicken kale Caesar and crispy wonton shrimp on rice that he ordered me. But while the food quells one hunger, another grows, until I find myself standing in the hallway in nothing but some Mayflower track pants, knocking on his door.

It opens just a crack. He's in a plain V-neck shirt and navy boxer briefs. When he sees it's me the door swings wider and he steps to the side so I can walk in. As the door closes behind me he looks down at my hand to see I'm holding the small vase of lavender.

"You don't like it? Does it make you sneeze or something?" Axel asks and his face pales. "Shit. I didn't even think about potential allergies. Do you need an antihistamine? Are you allowed to take those? Will they show up on a drug test? Or make you drows—"

I kiss him because, Jesus, Joseph, and Mother Mary, I need him to shut up. It takes him a minute but he starts kissing me back, opening his mouth, and meeting my tongue with his own. It's a languid kiss, and it takes the edge off the pointed emotional parts of this day.

"I like the lavender," I reply when we finally break apart and I take a breath. "I brought it with me because I kind of want to sleep here and I didn't want to skip the aromatherapy part of the night that you put together for me."

"Oh," Axel blinks those bottomless brown eyes. God, I swear I can see my own soul in them. He smiles, it's little but it's everything. "Okay."

"Okay? I can stay?"

He nods. "Of course."

"Because..." God I am so needy right now I want to crawl out of my own skin. I learned a very long time ago I wouldn't survive long if I cared what other people thought. So why does this man's opinion matter so much all of a sudden? Why do I desperately want him to tell me that I can stay because he wants me here, and not because it's part of this damn job.

"Because you want to be here. With me," he replies, and he gently takes the vase of lavender from me and walks it past his living area to his bedside table.

I follow along behind. He was obviously in the living room. There're rumpled cushions on the small couch and the nature show on the TV is low and his own, now-empty room service dishes are on the cart by the window. In the bedroom, after he puts the vase down, he turns slowly to face me. "I want you to be wherever you need to be to get in the zone for tomorrow."

I nod. It wasn't exactly the answer I was longing for. But it isn't horrible either. Nico's little tidbits about Axel's life bounce around my brain.

"Where are you going to live after this? And work?" I ask and his eyes move away from my face, down to the small scrap of carpet between our bare feet.

"After this, what?" he asks softly.

"After the season ends, or this woman's claims get proven false and my dad and Damien decide we don't have to do *this* anymore." I wait for him to look at me, or answer. Preferably both. But for several long minutes I get neither. And I fucking hate it. I reach up and hold his chin between my thumb and forefinger, tilting it up until our eyes meet. "Just tell me whatever you're thinking, Axel. It's fine. I promise."

I am lying like a goddamn rug.

"I have some ideas of what might be next," Axel says finally. "But if you want me to be honest, I'm not so sure about my game plan anymore. All I do know is that I hope it isn't Damien or your dad who decides when we don't do *this* anymore. I hope it's you. And me. I want it to be us that decides if and when this ends."

Every muscle in my body loosens, and that knot of melancholy that was writhing and twisting painfully in my chest melts away like the rubber off my tires when I spin out. And fuck, yeah I am spinning out right now. I've lost complete control over my feelings for this man, and I don't even care.

I let my hand slip from his chin, then across his jaw and back around his neck, my fingers threading into that thick, dark hair of his. "I like that. A lot. It's up to us. Just us."

And then I kiss him as I push him back towards his bed.

I WAKE up the next morning being spooned by Axel and his naked, perfect warm and solid body and feeling like I'm already the biggest winner on the planet. And then the universe said hold my beer.

The race, to be blunt, was an absolute nightmare. On the very first lap I narrowly avoid getting caught up in the collision between James and Spencer Samuels, my teammate's younger brother, because it happens directly in front of me. I take some wing damage from it but can keep going, and only drop to sixth. By lap nine I have to come in and fix the wing. I drop again, but only to ninth. After a few DRS attempts I get past the driver in eighth and then breeze by Samantha in seventh. Then, thanks to the driver in sixth spinning out and tapping a wall, and then Grady dropping out with engine trouble, I'm comfortably in fifth. Fucking fifth!

But on lap thirty the tires are all but gone. I keep telling Pablo that I have to come in. That the tires are dead. He keeps telling me I have to wait. I'm gritting my teeth, my hands shake with tension in every turn as I fight to keep the car on the track and then, I get passed and there isn't a damn thing I can do about it.

"Pablo. I need to fucking pit. Now!" I growl into the radio.

"Fine. Yes. Now. Do it now. Pit."

That should have been a relief. The answer. My chance at staying within points. If the team had managed a decent pit, getting me in and out with fresh tires in under two-and-a-half seconds, I would have come out in tenth and I could have held the position or even passed someone. But they didn't. When I slip into the pit, the mechanics swarm the car, the jack lifts me up, the tires are removed, and... nothing happens. Seconds tick by, everyone's heads move every which way like they're fucking bobbleheads, but no tires go on my car. For several agonizing, points-consuming seconds. Finally, in a burst of frantic movement new tires are slapped on, the jack drops me, and I roll back into the pit lane, cursing every swear word I can think of in two languages.

I finish twelfth. No points for the team. No points for me. No money. No nothing.

My blood is boiling as I get out of the car, after taking out my frustration on the steering wheel and my helmet, which I throw across the garage. The mechanics by my car all go still. I yank off as much of my gear as I can as I stalk over to the pit wall. My father is already there and I feel my chest get even tighter.

He's ranting at Pablo, on my behalf. And a lot of people are staring. I walk up beside him. "Save it," Pablo snaps at me before I even open my mouth. "I heard it all from your dad."

"No," I say sharply. "You didn't hear it all because you didn't hear it from me, your driver. The guy who just had his first points evaporate in front of his eyes because why? What the fuck happened?"

Pablo is about sixty, with a shock of pure white hair, wide-set brown eyes, and the wrinkled mouth of a man who smokes a pack a day. Right now there isn't a line on those lips because they are pressed so tight that you can barely make them out. "Listen, mistakes happen. You pushed to come in. We weren't ready. I explained this all to your dad and I'd rather let him tell you than waste my time repeating myself. Samuels made the podium. I'm going to go watch that. I'll email you later, okay?"

I watch him go but do nothing to stop it. Because, as usual, I know I'm not going to make him give a shit. I didn't podium. Samuels did. And that's all anyone here cares about. I turn and look at my dad. "Listen, I need you to do me a favor."

"I've already torn a stripe off Pablo and Bob is next. And that fucking lady mechanic too. I'm going to talk to them," Dad rants.

"It's strip, not stripe, and I'd prefer it if you did not," I say firmly. He jerks his head back a little bit so he can look me in the eye because I've got a couple inches on him.

Dad is looking exquisite as always, in clothes and shoes from his own label, a vintage Cartier on his wrist and classic ray-bans shoved up into his perfectly coiffed hair. I wish I had his casual sense of style but I don't think I do. It's never come easy, but I've never really had to try. He dressed me, like all parents do, when I was a kid. And as I got older, he's always sent over whatever he wanted me to wear to events. New clothes from his most recent line show up every season at my home. And when I'm not in Allard Couture, I'm in race gear. If left to my own devices, who knows what bad fashion choices I might make. He's gone out of his way to make sure I don't find out. I guess he feels the same way about my career choices too. And I guess I'm finally not okay with it.

"I love you. I respect you. And I know, trust me I do, that my ass is in this seat, with this team, because they wanted your cash, not my abilities behind the wheel," I tell him and he opens his mouth to object. "I don't care. I honestly don't. I mean... I care, but I am responsible for it. I let it happen this way. But I don't want your help now. Not like this."

"Like what?" he asks, his shoulders jutting back defensively as he crosses his arms in front of him. The sleeve pulls up on the wrist of his jacket and shirt and I see the only tattoo my father has. It's my birthdate in Roman numerals on the inside of his wrist. "Like you said it's my investment. My money. And their inability to find tires cost you points, which costs the team money and *you* money. Which is *my* money."

"Yeah. Okay, but *Papa...*" I sigh and shove a hand into my hair. It's gritty and damp from this hellish race. "Do you see any other investors here acting like a hooligan at a football match? You invested, they took your money and ran. They don't owe you, *Papa.* They owe me. They owe me the same level of respect and accountability they give Samuels. And they're never going to give it to me if you're always there demanding they give it to you."

For the first time in my life, my dad looks like I slapped him. I was never the teenager that talked back. Or the kid who threw tantrums. Oh, I caused plenty of trouble and drama but it was never directed *at* him. But now I'm talking back and even if I'm right, he's too wounded to see it.

"Fine." It's clearly anything but fine. He turns and starts walking away. "I'm flying to Paris tonight. See you at the end of the break."

"*Papa!*" I call but he keeps walking. "I was planning on taking my break in Paris too."

"Your plans changed when you got committed in Vegas." The way he words that should be funny, but I don't have time to laugh. "You will be on your commitment-moon. With your partner."

He marches away and I stand there staring after him with my mouth hanging open so wide I swear my chin is brushing the steamy asphalt.

What the fuck is a commitment-moon?

THERE ARE WORSE PLACES to have to spend eight days than cruising the Greek islands on a giant yacht. Naked. With a man who never fails to make you see stars when you come. But I'm not there at this exact moment, unfortunately. I'm on the island of Corfu, trying to pay attention while Gabriel gives an interview to a Sky Sports reporter. Damien lined it up. They do these puff pieces on all the drivers, a way for the fans to get a glimpse of their real lives off the track.

Before we got off the yacht to do the interview, Gabriel told me that he didn't think he was getting a segment with Sky this year because the season was nearing an end and no one had lined one up. He swears it's only because he's 'married' that they want one so he makes me come with him for it.

And he makes me wear a butt plug.

"Should we sit here?" the reporter asks, motioning toward a small table at the edge of a cafe overlooking the aquamarine water of the marina below.

They've just spent twenty minutes walking through the trails of a nature park, I look like the exertion from the easy meander is doing me in, but really, it's the plug in my ass that's causing me to sweat and almost pant.

"Sure." Gabriel pulls out a chair and motions for me to take a seat.

I give him a brief, but scalding glare and then plaster a smile on my face. "You know what? The breeze is lovely. I'm just going to stand here and enjoy it while you two finish up."

Gabriel grins. I begin to plot my lover's death, which I'll initiate moments after I come. Because fuck, do I need to come.

"Okay, *mon amour*," Gabriel replies airily, eyes dancing because he knows exactly what he's doing to me. "You enjoy that breeze."

He sits and the reporter sits down in the other chair and I move to the left, so I'm not in the camera's shot and then stand perfectly still, closing my eyes and thinking of that video I was shown in ninth-grade biology of two kangaroos mating. It was gross, and it's the only thing keeping my dick at half-mast.

They talk about a lot of stupid things, like what Gabriel does in his free time, does he have a favorite piece from his dad's designs, and what he'll do when his driving career ends. "I haven't given it much thought. I'm at the beginning of something. It feels like I'd be robbing myself of the joy of it if I was already thinking about the end."

Wow, that candid remark hits me like a freight train. I always think about the end. What I'll do next. What my backup plan is if something goes wrong. I remember when I got the condo and those keys were in my hand for the first time, I thought of what it would be like to hand them over to someone else. And now, I'm living that. It sucks, so why did I think of that, way back then, when I should have just been enjoying the moment?

"Can I get a happy couple shot? For B roll in the piece?" the reporter asks as they both stand up and shake hands. "Fans will love seeing you here with him."

I look at Gabriel, who is removing his mic. He hands it to the reporter and nods. "Okay. Sure."

I walk over and stand next to Gabe who wraps his arm around my shoulders. Behind us is the sea, dazzling and beautiful. I awkwardly stick both hands in my pockets and lean into Gabe.

"Great. Now look at each other and make small talk while I pan over and get the boats behind you too," The camera guy says.

Gabe tilts his head and leans in, so his lips are by my ear. "I know how uncomfortable press makes you, which is why I decided to give you a distraction."

"You'll be the death of me," I whisper back, a strained smile on my mouth as my eyes track the camera guy and the reporter also watching us, but too far away to pick up sound.

He grins up at me, all mischief and sex appeal. The cameraman stops recording. "Done guys. Thanks."

The reporter walks over to shake our hands one last time. Gabe drops his arm from my shoulder, and as he leans in with his right hand for the handshake, he palms my ass with his left. The unexpected touch has me jumping and clenching my butt cheeks, which makes me groan. *Out. Loud.*

I immediately turn it into a cough to try and cover it up while Gabe heartily slaps my back. "Sorry, he swallowed a bug. My husband isn't a nature person. He doesn't even surf? And he's Australian? How obscene is that?"

"There's a lot of obscene things happening right now, baby, but my dislike of water sports isn't one of them," I mutter under my breath and watch Gabriel's grin grow as he waves goodbye to the Sky Sports people.

I turn to him, my eyes wild, I'm sure, but he can't see them because I have sunglasses on. "Boat. Now. Please."

Thank God it's not a very long commute. We practically race up the dock and onto the yacht. It's the most amazing boat I've ever stayed on, personally. It's even bigger than the yacht I met Gabriel on. Louis called in a favor with the Team Principal of Arete Racing. Xavier Castellano's family owns this beast, I guess. I have noticed that Louis hasn't called once since we've been here, and I think something is up with that. But I haven't figured out how to broach the subject with Gabriel. And right now, with a plug in my ass, I'm not about to, so I concentrate on scurrying down the maze of hallways to our bedroom.

Gabriel's already pulled his shirt off and is reaching for my belt buckle when I close the door. The room is big, with three porthole windows, patio doors to a private deck, a king-sized bed, gleaming wood everywhere, and a massive bathroom attached at one end. I drag my lips over the thick cords of muscle in his neck. I love his neck so damn much. "Are you ready for me?"

His words vibrate up the column of his neck, against the press of my lips, and my cock jerks in my boxer briefs. He shoves my shorts down my legs. I slide my palms across his abs, circling his waist, pulling him to me. Why do I still have my fucking shirt on? "I'm ready and I'm so sensitive I might fucking come before you get inside."

"I can make sure that happens," he whispers as his lips ghost mine and he slips out of my embrace by sliding down my body.

Before I fully understand what's happening he's on his knees, my underwear is at my ankles with my shorts and his tongue is sliding up the underside of my shaft. I clench and my balls tingle and I tip my head back and grab his thick, luxurious hair like it's a life raft keeping me afloat.

After a few impossibly slow, incredible passes of his tongue, he looks up at me. The sunlight shooting through one of the round windows slices across his head, making his hair lighter, and the freckles that have come out in the sun, that pepper the bridge of his nose, are on display. "You're beautiful."

I shouldn't say it. It's silly and childish, but man, he is. Gabriel smiles softly and for the first time ever I think he is blushing. "You make me feel beautiful. That's a first."

And then he curls his fingers around my base and his other hand moves into the pocket of his shorts. His smile darkens as do his eyes as he adds, "And I think this is also a first."

The plug in my ass vibrates. I swear to God, I go blind. My knees start to give and I swear on a gasp. Gabriel bounces up and holds me up, pushing me back until my knees hit the side of the bed and I crumble onto it. My back arches. "Holy fuck. What the... oh God."

"See how good I was not turning that on while we were doing the interview?" Gabriel says and crawls over me. He's thankfully turned it off again. "People say I have no restraint. I'm all impulse and no control. This shows astounding control, don't you agree?"

I open my mouth but before words can make their way out, he's got the plug vibrating again and I am writhing and nothing that comes out of my mouth is discernible as a language. It feels fucking incredible and overwhelming. Gabriel slides down my body and takes my cock between his lips.

"You... I can't.. I'm... it's... Oh. *Oh.*"

I twist the sheets in my hands, slam my hips up, and come so hard down the back of Gabriel's throat he almost chokes. But he doesn't seem to mind. He pulls back a little, milks my shaft with his gentle grip, and swallows every hot drop.

The plug goes blissfully still and as I quiver and moan, Gabriel rolls my limp body over and I feel his hand between my cheek and then a void, as he pulls the plug from my body. He crawls back up, laying down beside me, and I roll into him so we're face-to-face. I reach for the button on his shorts. My hands are weak and shaky like the rest of me so I'm not making quick work of them. He huffs out a little laugh. "You can rest. This isn't a race, Axe. I have enough of those in my life."

"I want to make you come too," I insist and press our mouths together for a soft, gentle kiss. "And I'm open for business. Wouldn't want to waste that."

He laughs again and I know it's because my brash words have the flush of my cheeks getting darker. He glides a thumb pad over my cheek. "This was about you. Not me."

"I want it to be about us," I reply and finally get his damn shorts undone. "I like being the reason you come."

"But you're going to be sensitive. It might not be pleasurable."

"That's never a possibility where you're involved. Trust me." I find the energy to sit up and tug his shorts and underwear down to his knees. His perfect dick is rock hard and leaking. "I want you inside me."

Gabriel exhales in a shudder as I drag my fingers over his shaft before reaching for the pack of condoms that have been a permanent fixture on the nightstand. We don't bother to hide them from the staff or anyone. This is our commitment-moon, after all.

Ten minutes later he's finally all the way in. It took a while because he was right, I may be stretched but my nerve endings are like live wires. I feel every movement, every inch of him, more than I ever have before. But I'm not complaining.

We're facing each other, my legs bent on either side of his trim waist, knees up by his shoulders. He's holding himself up, off of me a little. "Are you okay?"

I nod because words are failing me again. He starts to move, gently, slowly, and I swear that makes it worse, so I grab his hips and set his rhythm. Not exactly blinding but faster while still being gentle somehow. My dick is growing between us, like some kind of miracle. I have never been one to get hard so quickly after an orgasm. Another part of me Gabriel brings out that I didn't think existed.

He sees my erection and immediately lowers his torso so all of his belly is against mine, creating this amazing pressure and friction against my cock. I start moving my hips too and he pants out, "I'm not going to last long."

"I don't need you to." He twists his hips, bottoms out, and hits my sweet spot.

Oh fucking hell, how is this better than perfect?

Gabriel comes with a lewd moan and whatever's left in me releases too. I, true to form, don't linger in the magic of my second orgasm. I'm already thinking about the end of our sequestered time on this yacht and dreading it.

I DON'T KNOW if I blacked out or fell asleep, but when my eyes open again, the horizon out the portholes is streaked with purples and I'm alone. I sit up, there's the scent of lavender and mint in the room, which is the body wash Gabriel has started using since this trip began, and the air is a little steamy so I know he showered. I have no idea where he is but he won't be gone long, he left his phone on the night table. As I pull back the covers a text alert lights up the screen and, without thinking, I read the first few words.

It's from Damien. It starts with:

> Your father asked me to set up a meeting for...

I head into the bathroom and shower, wondering why Damien is setting up meetings for Louis with his son. Louis and Gabriel used to text each other all the time. And Louis called Gabriel, like the old-school man he is, at least once a day while we were together during the race weeks, but he hasn't called once since we came to Greece. And I don't think they've messaged either.

I walk out of the shower and back into the bedroom to find Gabriel stretched out on the chaise lounge under the windows. He sits up and grabs the plate he's got in front of him when I enter. It's filled with melon and ham and cheese and a cut-up loaf of crusty white bread. "I figured we could have *apero* on the deck. The sunset is kind of amazing."

Gabriel explained to me when this trip started that *apero* was the shortened version of the French word for *aperitif*, which is the evening hour the French partake in snacks and a cocktail. We've been doing it every night of this trip and I kind of love it. I nod and throw on a pair of shorts and underwear. He's not wearing a shirt so I don't bother either. I follow him out the patio doors onto the deck. He's right. The pink and purple streaks I saw when I woke up have darkened and the sky is like a Jackson Pollock painting.

"Stunning," I remark, and he hands me a glass of sangria he poured from the pitcher filled with ice that's on the small table between two lounge chairs. He must have set this up while I was showering.

He pours his own and we clink glasses. Gabriel gives me a tsk sound. "Do it again and look me in the eyes or it's bad luck."

I chuckle but follow orders, making sure I'm staring into those perfect navy eyes but I also frown like it's a hardship. That makes him grin. He loves when I give him attitude. "Is this superstitious stuff because you're an athlete?"

"It's because I'm French," he replies. "At least this one is."

After a sip of the cocktail, I drop into a lounge chair and tug on his hand until he's sitting on it too, between my legs, his back pressed into my front. We watch the sunset in silence. He reaches back and pops a piece of ham-covered melon into my mouth before taking his own piece.

"Have you heard from your dad lately?" I ask, hoping it sounds casual.

"Nope."

"Is he giving us space so our fake honeymoon is just about us?" I hope the joke sounds funny. I'm not good at this—prying, snooping, whatever.

"No he's pouting," Gabriel replies. "I told him I don't want him to handle any race situations anymore. I want to deal with the issues I have with my crew, their bungled pit stops, and whatever else."

"Oh. Okay." I take another sip of sangria and run my hand over his head. His hair is still damp from his own shower, which I'm sad I slept through.

He turns his head, the grate of his unshaven cheek tickling my nipple. "Okay? As in okay you think I made the right decision?"

Our eyes connect. He looks more vulnerable than I have ever seen him and it makes my heart feel fragile and also too big for my chest. God, this man, with all his hard, devil-may-care attitude, actually cares what I think. And I owe it to him to be honest. I pick my words carefully. "I think it's the right decision. If you actually do intend to handle it."

His eyelashes flutter and he sits up. He puts his drink down on the little table beside us and turns sideways so he can look at me better. I don't like the distance it puts between us, physically. It feels like emotional distance too. "You don't think I'll handle it?"

"I think you're more than capable of handling anything," I reply and drop a hand onto the inside of his exposed thigh, on the leg closest to me which is bent and resting on the chaise. "You know how talented you are, and that with or without your dad's money you deserve to be behind the wheel in F_1. But you don't make others see that. I mean, you do with your driving, but when they stupidly choose to ignore that. Well, you've let them. This whole season."

"I know but I've decided not to anymore." Gabriel moves a little like he's going to stand up, and that means he's closer to walking away and I hate that idea.

So I hook my hand on his thigh behind that bent knee and give it a little tug. I pull his leg so it's hanging down the other side of the lounge chair, forcing his whole body to turn to face me. His brow furrows a little bit but he keeps talking. "I saw the way you looked at me when you found out how little the team interacts with me. Helps me. Cheers me on. And I felt like... well, I mean if you're looking at me like that, then everyone else is too. From the fans to the reporters to the other teams. And while there is something to be said for not giving a flying fuck what other people think, there's also..."

"A fine line between not caring what they think and looking like you don't care at all, about anything," I suggest, and he nods.

"I do care. About a lot of things. Including my career." Gabriel's voice is soft and vulnerable, and my heart is seriously going to impale itself on my rib cage it feels so big now.

I put my sangria down beside the chair and grab his hips, pulling him toward me. "Come here."

I jostle him until he is on my thighs, straddling my lap, facing me. He delves his fingers into my hair, raking them from temples to the back of my head and then he dips his head until our foreheads touch. "I'm going to demand strategy meetings. In person. I'm going to hold them accountable for everything. I'm out there giving this my all and I should get the same back. And then, when I start earning points, and my reputation gets cleared from this woman's lies, and other teams dare to notice me... I'm going to sign with someone else. Fuck Mayflower."

I smile. "Fuck Mayflower."

Gabe kisses me, and I kiss him back for so long that the colors in the sky fade to gray and the solar-powered deck lights flicker on. Gabriel holds the back of my neck and I feel the cool hard metal of his commitment ring. "No matter how the season goes, or what happens with the accusations or Mayflower, I'm one proud husband. You know that, right?"

Gabriel bites his bottom lip and looks away, but I catch a glimpse of the smile on his face before he does. "Shush now, or I'll make you wear the butt plug the entire day tomorrow. On Vibrate."

"Don't threaten me with a good time," I laugh. "By the way, your phone got a text earlier. You left it by the bed."

He nods. "Who was it?"

"Damien."

"Ah *merde*. I should answer him." Gabriel sighs and walks into our bedroom.

I stretch out on the lounger. It's dark but the air is still warm and carries that heavy scent of salt that has always created a light feeling inside me when I inhale it, even on my heaviest days. Today, despite the emotional minefields that could have gone off, has been a really good day. Gabriel isn't like anyone I've ever dated. He's so forthright about his wants and needs. He doesn't play games or gaslight or make me responsible for his emotions. It's... terrifyingly unfamiliar. Everyone, from my sister to Billy, has told me I settle for too little when I date. Eric drove that point home in spades. And I walked into this attempt to rebuild my life with the mantra that I would 'hold out for more' but deep down I wasn't actually sure if more existed. And worse still, I was worried that it just didn't exist for me. After all, there had to be a reason that men repeatedly treated me like garbage, right?

But as I lie here on this plush lounger, floating on the Aegean sea, my ass sore and my heart full, I realize that it does exist —that something more—and not every man will treat me like garbage. I realize I have everything I wasn't sure was real, in this fake relationship. And it's time I take the leap that Gabe's taking. It's time I tell him what I really want and how I really feel. I think... I'm actually kind of sure that he will want it to. That he wants me. Us. For real.

I pull myself off the lounger and turn to the bedroom to make this real, officially. But he's standing there, his phone dangling from his hand. His eyes sharp and serious. Even in the moonlight, I can see the tan tone his skin has taken on during this trip has suddenly faded. He's pale.

"What?"

"There's been a development. With the case," Gabriel says, his voice flat but uneven. "We have a meeting in Paris the day after tomorrow."

Oh shit.

Eminem lyrics about sweaty palms, vomit, and spaghetti rumble about in my head, distracting me from the sights of Paris that roll by outside the window. The bustling cafes, the breathtaking architecture, the Eiffel Tower. Axel sits on the seat next to me. Our hands are laced together, the back of mine against the supple black leather of the seat.

We haven't talked much about what may or may not come from this meeting. It's the first sit-down with the opposing counsel and it wasn't supposed to happen until the season was over. All Damien will say is that it was his decision to move it up, and he assures they've got this in the bag so no sense dragging it out. Dad isn't saying anything and I'll be damned if I'm going to be the first one to text. I did nothing wrong. I wasn't even harsh. I was honest. Still, there is a small, hard stone of guilt in my gut that I refuse to acknowledge.

The trip from Greece to Paris was seamless. We landed at Charles de Gaulle last night around seven and I took Axel back to my apartment in the Marais and we ordered take-out, watched Netflix, and had sex on my couch. And then in my bed. He's quiet, but I don't need him to fill me up with a bunch of words that mean nothing. I just need him here, with me. And he is. Despite the orders.

He turned to me this morning, while I was shaving and he was getting dressed and held up his phone. "Damien just sent me an email. I have the day off. With pay, he says."

"His way of making sure you don't come to the meeting," I tell him. I'm not an idiot. I know it's not appropriate to bring my boyfriend to a legal proceeding like he's an emotional support animal, but he kind of is. And that's why I did ask him to come, for the ride there, and to hang out in the area and meet me right after. And he agreed. Before the email.

"You don't have to come now."

"Why? Because you don't need me?" Axel asks.

Because you're not being paid to be there, I thought but didn't say. It's so unlike me to filter my words that I feel like I'm having an out-of-body experience. Until Axel walks up behind me and wraps one of his muscular arms around my shoulders, pinning my back to his front. Our eyes meet in the bronze-framed mirror over my antique vanity. "Because I wasn't going for the paycheck, Gabe."

"I still want you there."

He nods, kisses my cheek, and walks back into the bedroom to get dressed. And now he's getting out of the Uber with me, stepping into the muggy Paris fall air and smiling down at me. "Text at any point. For any reason. I won't be far."

"Where are you going?"

He shrugs his broad shoulders. "We're near Champs Elysees," he says, his Australian accent positively butchering the iconic street name. "I won some cash at a casino a couple weeks ago so I might treat myself. Or just window shop because frivolous purchases make me nauseous."

I laugh and lean in and kiss him chastely. When we part he

starts down the street and I walk into the building where my father, his lawyer, and my fate awaits.

My dad, surprisingly, is the one waiting for me when I get off the elevator. He's looking as sharp and cool as ever in a beige suit with a blue shirt and, most importantly, a smile. "How have you been?"

I hug him because it hits me how much this little rift has bothered me. He hugs me back, tightly, and pats my shoulder. "You haven't answered my question."

"I'm okay," I tell him. "I'm worried about this. I know Damien said it was a good sign but..."

"It is," Dad assures me and then clears his throat. "Axel didn't come with you?"

"Damien told him not to." My dad's eyes widen and his jaw flexes for a minute. He turns to look down the hall. Through a glass wall at the end, I can see Damien, he's pouring a coffee from a carafe and chatting with a shorter blonde woman. "You didn't know that?"

"No, I didn't," Dad replies, clearing his throat, and hits me with a fatherly stare. "Was Greece... fun?"

"We were a perfect version of a committed couple," I promise. "Every time we saw a camera, and there were a few paps plus the Sky interview, we made sure we looked like we were madly in love."

We had started walking towards the conference room but when he speaks next my feet grind to a halt. "Was that hard? Looking like you're in love? Or is it just the way things are?"

He stops now too, when he realizes I've fallen out of step with him, and he turns to catch my eye over his shoulder. His smile is soft and curious, not judging or angry. My dad has known I was bi since I was fifteen. I told him over dinner. A fancy dinner at his favorite restaurant in Paris, La Coupole. I just said, "I think boys are attractive as well as girls." And he nodded and said, "Fine." And that was that. So what he's curious about here isn't my sexuality. It's whether this thing he arranged has grown roots.

"Louis. Gabriel." Damien's head pokes its way out of the open conference room door. "She's on her way up with her lawyer. Let's get settled, shall we?"

I start walking again, entering the room with a stiff nod to everyone, and let Dad lead me to a seat on one side of the long dark wood table. Damien is next to him and the blonde, who pulls out a laptop, is beside me. I haven't seen Dominique Lambert since she walked off the private plane that night. She was still employed by Dad at that point. She'd screwed up his travel arrangements to the Miami Fashion Week, which was why he had to fly us all private, which he hates doing due to climate issues. She'd apparently screwed up a bunch of other stuff, which is why she was let go fourteen days after the flight. And she accused me five days after that.

She looks similar but not the same as I remember. She's paler, which is strange after the summer. She's got her brown hair pulled back in a tight bun and she doesn't seem to be wearing much make-up. She used to be the queen of bright lipstick. Her suit looks like it's a little big. She keeps her eyes down as she enters the room after her lawyer and they sit across from us.

"I'm still unclear as to why we had to meet in person," her lawyer says swiftly in French. "If you're looking for a settlement, I could have given you a figure over the phone."

Damien smirks. It's a cold, hollow look on him. Not scary or intimidating just... mean. I glance at Dominique, who looks at me directly and then down at her folded hands. "We wanted you to see this in person so we can be certain you understand the gravity."

Damien is also speaking French, but his is broken since it's his second language. He's originally German. I think. He motions to the woman beside me. She is ready, immediately moving her laptop so it's at the top of the table for all of us to see, and clears her throat. "What you and your client are unaware of is that some private companies use cameras in the cabin."

"They aren't always turned on, and some clients request that they stay off during a flight," Damien explains. "And they don't cover every inch of the interior."

"But lucky for us, they cover the kitchen area," the blonde lady says. "And they were on."

She hits a button and footage of the galley kitchen on the private plane appears. It's grainy and black and white but it's good enough. You can clearly see Dominique standing there making tea, and I walk in and stand beside her. I browse through the candy selection and it's clear I'm talking to her, but there's no audio. And then there's a rumble of turbulence. We both grab the counter. The look on my face gets serious. She looks panicked. And then it's like we are suddenly in a bouncy castle. Everything in the kitchen from the tea bags to the snacks to the tea in her mug jerks up suddenly and then down, very fast. I pitch forward and reach for anything to keep me from face-planting. She lurches sideways, hitting the counter with her arm. She grabs for me at the very same time I grab for her. Her hand hits my elbow and mine hits her bicep, but when she falls sideways, it moves to her chest. It's so quick and grainy on the video you can barely see it. My hand is gone, back on her arm instantly, and I keep her from tumbling to the ground entirely.

The turbulence stops, we straighten, and you can see my lips moving. I remember asking her if she was okay, her nodding, and then telling her we should sit down and following her out of the kitchen.

The screen goes black. The blonde dramatically snaps the laptop closed. "We have a team of techs working on slowing down the footage and a lip reader ready to transcribe every word they said, including Ms. Lambert thanking Mr. Allard. Repeatedly."

"This... this could be fake," the lawyer stutters.

"We have people working to prove it's not," Damien announces and then he shrugs. "We are perfectly willing to give you a copy to analyze yourself."

Dominique has her eyes down. "I'm... I would like to leave."

She starts to move her chair back. Damien stands abruptly and his voice grows mean again. "Not yet. Not until you sign papers dropping all claims of harassment and return your severance."

My head spins to my dad. I'm thankful he looks just as baffled as I am. Dad clears his throat. "Damien..."

Damien smiles, proudly, at my father. Like he thinks that's something we want. Dad stands too. Dominique finally looks up at me. "I'm sorry. It was never about you. I... worked very hard for your father and it was never enough. And I admit I struggled. My mom died the year I got the job and maybe I wasn't ready for so much pressure. I could have done better but I was angry he let me go. My severance was nothing. Paris is so expensive and I didn't want to move back to Bayonne and have to tell my whole family I failed. I just... I'm sorry. But the severance is gone. It was gone months ago."

"Dominique..." Her lawyer shakes his head and starts packing up his belongings. He didn't care about her struggle at all. He only saw her as a paycheck and now that it's clear the payday isn't coming he has no urge to stick around. "I'll be sending you my bill."

He marches out without another word, and Dominique steps closer to the table. "What do I have to sign?"

Damien smugly shoves a piece of paper toward her and hands her a pen, which she takes with shaking hands. I lean forward to stare down the table at my father, pleading. He nods. "I know, *mon coeur*." Dad stands up. "Dominique, we will *not* be requiring the return of the severance. This ends here. Now. And we all go our separate ways."

"And I'll pay your legal fees," I add.

"No!" Damien barks, like he has any kind of power over me.

"It's not an admission of guilt," I say calmly, my eyes searching out my father's because he's the only approval I require. "I trust Ms. Lambert will see this as a simple act of kindness and also keep it private."

"I... I don't expect you to help me," She sputters out, her eyes watering. "But if you did... I will never forget such generosity. I don't deserve it."

"You made a mistake. Email me directly and we'll take care of it," My father says.

I glare at him and he clears his throat. "I'll pass the information on to Gabriel to handle."

"Thank you," she says meekly, then she finishes signing and shoves the paper back at Damien. She glances at me again. "I'm sorry, again."

She leaves. And I pull my phone from my pocket to text Axel.

It's over. She's dropping everything.

OMG amazing. I'm so happy for you!

Before I can respond, Damien adds, "All that's left now is releasing the tape. Oh and moving Axel into his new position."

My phone buzzes.

Do you want me to come back now and meet you? I can be there in ten.

"Release the tape? Of the plane? Why? To who?" Louis asks.

"And move Axel where?" I croak out.

Damien is looking at both of us like we're dim-witted. Like we're missing a very obvious plot hole. "We release the tape to the media. I mean, yes, it's great she dropped everything but the world is pessimistic and everyone is going to think she was paid off or something. No one is going to believe Gabriel is innocent unless we give them the definitive proof."

"But everyone is already focused on him and Axel. Won't those pessimistic people just assume the tapes are fake or whatever anyway?" Dad argues.

"Where is Axel moving?" I ask again, louder this time.

"To London. He took this fake boyfriend gig because we guaranteed him an executive position in our UK division," Damien says. "You didn't think there wasn't something in it for him, did you?"

I feel... sick.

Dad stands up again. "Gabriel, what are your thoughts? On releasing the tapes."

I stand up too, but my knees feel weak. My phone buzzes in my pocket again. I ignore it, knowing it's Axel, and turn to Dad. Despite the pain in my chest and the emotional whiplash of everything that's been revealed today, I can see the olive branch he's extending here. He's not just trying to fix my life for me. He's giving me the chance to make the decisions that affect me. I swallow. There's a lump. "I think that she doesn't need to get canceled on top of everything else. And I don't need to prove anything. I didn't do it. People who matter know that. I just... I want this all to end. All the *merde*. And I need some air."

I walk around the conference table, pausing to kiss my father's cheek. "*Je t'aime.* I'll call you later."

"Talk to him, Gabriel," Dad whispers, rubbing my arm. "Let him tell you his side."

I nod, but I don't know if I'll have the guts to do it. Right now I just want to walk away. From everything and everyone. And never look back.

HE'S NOT ANSWERING my texts. It's been twenty-nine minutes since he saw my last one, but he didn't respond. I walk back to the building where he had his meeting and decide I'll linger outside for as long as I have to. But Gabe doesn't come out, Damien does.

"Hi," I say, coming to stop next to him as he digs in his pocket for a lighter for the cigarette dangling from his lips.

"Oh. Hi. I thought I said you had the day off," Damien replies and flicks his lighter. He closes his eyes as he inhales so he misses the frown on my face, which I quickly remove.

"I know. I'm looking for Gabe."

"Gabriel? Yeah. He left about half an hour ago," Damien replies. "The case is over. Done. No more accusations. Oh, and you've got the job in London. I assume someone from Louis' team will reach out with a start date. I'll get the paperwork ready. You have to sign another NDA. For the new position."

Is he serious? Does he honestly think I still want the job in London? Wait. I don't? What the hell am I going to do for work? I'm not going to be paid to be Gabriel's fake partner anymore.

As I stand there having an existential crisis on the Parisienne sidewalk, Damien blows smoke in my face and points to my hand. "And you don't have to wear that thing anymore. Although I guess they may need you at one more race... I don't know. An abrupt break-up might be a bit much. Yeah, one more race. Maybe you finish out the season? I'll have a meeting about it with the team. I'll call you."

He starts down the street, but calls back, "You did a good job, Walsh. Maybe a little too much... gusto. But yeah. It worked."

He leaves and I pull my phone out of my pocket to stare at the last text I sent Gabriel. Is that why he's not responding? Because this nightmare smear case is done and he doesn't need me anymore? Oh God, how stupid was I to actually fall for him? I was going to tell him too. Of course, he was just using me. I was there to be used. This isn't his fault.

I walk aimlessly down the unknown street. I don't know where I am or where I'm going. Tourists snap pictures and locals bustle by with purpose. The early fall sun is making all the monuments and the Seine golden but I'm drowning in my own inner conflict and can't admire any of it.

I try to see a bright side. I'm going to be the Head of UK Public Relations for Allard Couture. I can hold my head up high. Eric will hear the news. My old clients will. I'll have risen from the ashes like a Phoenix. No one played me or used me this time. I worked the system to my advantage. So why do I feel like I might punch something or cry?

My phone buzzes. When I see Gabriel's name tears do swim in my eyes. But they're tears of relief, not pain.

> Sorry. I got... overwhelmed. I walked home.
> Can you grab an Uber back?

I text him back a thumbs up and pull up the car app on my phone.

On the ride over, Gabriel texts me the code for his building so I don't have to buzz him to get in. I ride the tiny elevator to his floor and knock softly on his door. "*Ouvert!*"

His voice is so sexy when he speaks French. It gets velvety and smooth. I turn the handle and walk inside and the smile that was toying with the corners of my mouth disappears when I see him. He's just past the entryway, in the living room. He's standing perfectly still, his jacket off and his tie hanging loosely. His sleeves are rolled up and his belt is undone. His socks and shoes are off and his face... is pale. Even the freckles.

"I saw Damien. He said it went well. This doesn't look well," I say as I walk toward him.

He nods, and his eyes dart away from mine. "They found video. It proves my side of the story. She signed paperwork to drop everything."

"Great!" I say, but the enthusiasm in my voice doesn't reach my body. I feel cold and kind of anxious like there is a shoe that still has to drop. Or maybe an atomic bomb.

"Yeah. Great. For my career and yours, right?" Gabriel smiles but it doesn't reach his eyes and there isn't one degree of warmth in it. "Allard Couture's new Director of UK Public Relations."

He starts to clap. Slowly. It echoes around the apartment mockingly.

"Gabe."

"So when do you leave?" Gabriel asks. He runs a hand through his hair, sending it askew, and then turns to the window. It's wide open and the curtains, which are a gauzy white fabric, are blowing a little bit. "I don't get to London much. I hear it's great though. Henri called and he wants to talk 'exit strategy' but I don't think we need to make this formal. I mean hell, we kind of went off-script already. Might as well just write our own ending too. You can leave whenever it suits you."

I walk closer. His living room faces a courtyard. Somewhere in another apartment with its windows open someone is playing the piano. The sound of the music wafts up and into the air around us. "I should have told you about that part of the deal."

"You didn't do anything wrong."

"I didn't," I agree and let my fingers brush his hairline at the back of his neck. He steps away, moving across the room, putting the couch between us. "But I still should have told you. Truth is I haven't thought about it much."

He nods. "Yeah. I mean there's been a lot going on. Well, I wanted to say I appreciate all you've done. And how you made this arrangement fun. It probably would have been unbearable with someone else."

Is he really doing this?

"You're welcome?" I say it because it sounds as absurd as what he's saying.

We stare at each other, silently, with nothing but faint piano chords as the soundtrack to this break-up. But can it really be a break-up if it was never real? His phone chirps. Breaking our staring contest, he snatches it off the end table and looks at it. Then he strides over to the dining room and grabs his suit jacket. "We have to pack and leave." He holds up his phone before tucking it in his pocket. "The car is taking us to the airport in forty minutes."

"We're leaving now?"

"Yeah. I have to be on the other side of France for the GP tomorrow." Gabriel sighs and rubs his forehead like he has a headache. "And we have to fly commercial. I can't pick the times."

"And you want me to come?"

He stiffens at that question. "We're still playing this game, aren't we? Or do you want to just vanish? The press will ask questions either way so, like I said, up to you."

"I'm not asking if my services are still required," I reply, trying hard not to feel like he's gaslighting me. He isn't... not really. He's just hurt. I think. "I am asking if *you* want me there."

I watch his shoulders fall on a deep exhale. His tough guy, cool, dauntless image is gone now. He looks positively broken. "This is all so fucked and I just... I don't know if we can unfuck it."

"We can," I promise blindly because even though I don't have a plan, I know that we have to fix this. We have to save the love that we created in the eye of the storm of lies.

"How?" Gabriel swallows.

"Answer my question."

The idea of this ending with Gabriel makes my insides cold and hollow, but I wait for him to decide. I'm all in. Here's where I find out if I made yet another mistake when it comes to my heart. "I want you with me. In France, for the Grand Prix."

It's not everything, but it's something. "Okay. Let's go then."

"Okay."

We pack up what we brought to Paris silently, moving about the apartment like ghosts. The flight is much of the same. We're in Business, in sleeping pods beside each other but separate. I start digging nuggets of hope out of little things, like a miner sifting for gold. The fact that he doesn't put up the divider between our sleeping pods. The way he waits for me as I gather my things so we can debark the plane together. The way he doesn't allow me to stop at my hotel room door, instead, he wordlessly takes my hand and leads me to his. And most importantly how, even though we don't have sex, he doesn't push me away when I curl into his back, pressing my lips to his shoulder blade before falling into a restless sleep.

When Gabe leaves in the morning for press conferences and practice and all the things that start his race weekend, I wonder whether he realizes that he takes my heart with him. He'll always have it, even if he decides we can't unfuck this.

I GET MORE media attention than ever because it's considered my home GP. I'm French. Of course, the marriage and the statement released by Dominique that she was not pursuing any legal action anymore and that the whole thing was a misunderstanding, has everyone hounding me in all the press events. I keep with the canned answers. "I appreciate her setting the record straight and I am happy to move past this misunderstanding."

I say it so much it's hard not to yawn while doing it. In truth, I am very grateful it all worked out so easily. But I'm also still hurting from finding out Axel is moving to London. This whole relationship was based on a lie. I get that but now it feels like a lie based on a lie because he didn't tell me there was a job waiting for him. His reward for putting up a good front with me. I knew he was being paid, but I didn't know there was more to it.

"Are you ready?" Holly asks me and I nod.

I'm actually not ready to do this big sit-down piece with the docuseries. They've never wanted me before and I feel like this is still undeserved. I want them to want to interview me because

I'm driving well, which I am. But they only want me because my personal life has become interesting.

Holly puts a hand to her stomach. "Okay, so the basics. You can swear, they actually kind of like that. But remember, you represent the sport and your team so keep it relatively PG. Oh, and they will ask you about personal stuff. Don't get pissy like you usually do. Okay?"

"Okay."

She freezes. "I will be back in a jiffy." Then she sprints to the ladies' room which is at the end of the hall.

Jasper's interview finishes and he walks across the big room, directly to me. He isn't a talker. I mean, except to Cristian, but he stops in front of me. His bodyguard is a few feet behind him. I wonder what it's like to be a prince and need a bodyguard. "You ever wonder about the contradiction of having a bodyguard following you everywhere you go except in the one place where you're actually at imminent risk? The race car?"

Jasper narrows his eyes and then kind of shrugs. "No. But I'll be thinking about it now."

"Sorry. I'm in a philosophical mood."

"Why?" Jasper asks simply.

I decide to tell him because if anyone knows about confidentiality it's a gay prince and besides, I just need to vent to someone who will be unbiased. "Axel and I. That whole thing was fixed. It was arranged. To make my image softer and divert attention from the accusations."

He looks stunned. "The whole thing? Could have fooled me. Actually, you *did* fool me."

I smile sadly. "Yeah, I think I fooled me too. But he was doing it for a position with my dad's company. I didn't know that. As you might have heard, the accusations against me have been dropped. So he doesn't have to be my boyfriend anymore. Or at least he won't have to be soon."

"Wow." Jasper blinks.

"Sorry. I don't mean to unload on you." I look away. Watching the camera crew putter around their set moving cables is more tolerable than looking at the face of the virtual stranger-slash-co-worker I just spilled my guts to.

"I don't mind being an ear for you," Jasper says and runs a hand through his blond hair. "I could have used one when Cristian and I were starting out. Can I ask you a question? Where is Axel now?"

"He's at the hotel, I think."

"So he's here in France?" I nod and Jasper smiles. "And is it the fact that he took this job intending to get another job that's the problem? If he'd just taken the job with nothing lined up afterward, would that make you feel better?"

"Yes. No. I don't know." I rub the stubble on my jaw because I didn't bother to shave this morning. "It just feels like he had this prize he was going for all this time. Like maybe even when I thought it was about us, it wasn't."

"Has he said that?"

"No, but it feels that way."

Holly emerges from the bathroom but she's at the end of the hall patting her mouth with a napkin. My time with Jasper is coming to an end. He's going to clam up as soon as she's within earshot and I don't blame him. "Look, all I can say is people's intentions change," Jasper says, his eyes darting over to Holly as well. "When Cristian and I got together for the first time, I swear his only intention was to upset me. Throw me off my game. I think it was a joke to him. And my intention? Hell, I don't even know what it was but I can tell you with absolute certainty it was not to fall in love with him. But that's exactly what happened."

Huh. I sigh. He smiles and grips my shoulder, squeezing for a second. "Intentions, plans, what we think we want... it's fluid.

Like sexuality. Forget where you started. Have an honest conversation with each other about where you are now."

Jasper stiffens, like the royal iceman everyone thinks he is, and walks away, bodyguard in tow. Holly pops a breath mint in her mouth and waves me over to take the seat the crew is currently lighting.

The interview is a fluff piece. The questions are painfully banal. But then he asks me about the fine I got for not removing my ring. My fingers land on the band, pressing the cool metal into the tips. "Yeah. That was dumb. I understand it's for my safety I was just being... obstinate."

"Do you think that maybe you do that because you know your dad will always have your back? You've never had rules, have you? I mean, before F1?"

I shake my head. "My father was not a walk in the park. I had rules and curfews. And I was in karting for years and F2 and F3. I followed those rules just fine. I'm aware that my father is a safety net that some people may not have. Be it other drivers, or other bisexual men. I am lucky he accepts me and supports me in all my pursuits. But if we're being honest here, it's a hindrance too."

"How so?"

"You think I'm taken seriously? We both know I'm not." Somewhere in the back of my brain something is panicking and telling me to keep my mouth shut, but I don't. Typical Gabriel Allard, authentic to a fault. "Mayflower gave me the seat because he bailed them out. But they don't give me much else. The support isn't there. The team isn't behind me and you know what? That's fine. I am still laying it all out there. I'm still doing my best. One day soon I will get those points. And money. And I still won't get a fucking thing in return. And I'll still keep trying. If I'm lucky, someone will notice and offer me a contract somewhere else. Somewhere that wants *me*, not my dad's money. But even if it doesn't happen, I'll still keep proving them, and you, wrong. Even if no one wants to notice."

The producer is just staring at me. The camera stops rolling. I see the light go out, but no one moves. I stand up, a pleasant smile on my face because I feel good. I feel lighter like I lifted that chip off my shoulder all by myself. "Are we good?"

He nods.

"Thanks guys." I pluck off my mic, hand it to the sound girl, and leave.

I DON'T EVEN KNOW if I am allowed in Mirabella's paddock. My pass says all-access but like, could this be considered an act of treason because I'm dating Gabriel? But wait, am I dating Gabriel? I guess that's why I'm here. Because I don't know what the fuck I'm doing and I need my best friend.

"Axe!" Lucia belts out my name as she walks by the front doors. She pauses to punch my shoulder. She's not a big hugger or toucher, I've noticed. "Are you here to see Billy?"

"Yeah. Is that allowed?"

"Of course. I mean maybe not on race day. On race day we might have to lock you in a dungeon or something, but today, sure." Lucia winks and holds open the door for me. "He should be in his room. Last door on the left."

She points down the hallway and then starts up the stairs. I wave goodbye to her and head down the hall. Sure enough, there is a little plaque on the second door on the left that says Billy James. I rap my knuckles on the door. "Yep?"

I swing it open. Billy is sitting on a chair, his trainer in front of him, pulling on a larger rubber training band that is around the side of Billy's head while he uses the muscle in his neck to pull on it in the other direction. My neck cramps just watching this and I reach up and rub it.

"Okay. Done," the trainer says. I don't know his name. Billy's normal trainer, for most of his career, is a girl named Clara that I know really well. But she quit at the end of last season and now he's got this nerdy-looking guy.

Billy fist-bumps the trainer and turns to me. "I heard Gabe is free and clear."

"Yep. Great news."

"Yep." Billy waits until the trainer steps out and closes the door. Then he turns his big blue eyes back to me. "So... what does that mean for you?"

"It means that Louis and Damien, the shit stain that works for him, are going to end the relationship. And I'm supposed to trot off to London for my cushy new job. The one that I wanted so badly it got me into this mess and, in the words of Porky Pig, 'that's all folks'."

Billy nods. Then he stands up and rubs his chin while pinching his eyebrows together. It means he's pretending to think deeply about something. It's sarcastic acting as he once explained to me. "So... how do you think they'll end you guys? You cheat? He finds out you have a secret baby with a dingo in Australia? You were already married to someone else? What lie will they tell the public next?"

He's trying to be funny but I don't laugh. Neither does he. "I'll probably just disappear with nothing more than a press release. Mr. Allard and Mr. Walsh have decided to go their separate ways, but they wish each other the best in all they do and remain friends. That's how I'd do it if I were running the show. It's how I *have* done it for a bunch of other people."

I drop down onto the small couch in his dressing room and close my eyes, pinching the bridge of my nose.

"Okay, look, I have to be in a practice session in twenty

minutes so let me just tell you what you need to hear," Billy announces, spinning his chair around and straddling it so he can lean his chest on the back while he faces me. "Gabe is not Eric. He isn't using you. He has never gaslighted you. He thinks you are the moon and the stars and the fucking sun. I can not only see it in the way he looks at you but also in the way he treats you. And you... yeah, you wanted the job. Who wouldn't want the fucking job? But now you want Gabe too. And it's okay to want both."

"The job feels dirty now," I admit. "I mean, it was this reward for something that turned out not to be a job. Taking it feels, disingenuous. And like it cheapens this thing with Gabe."

"It cheapens nothing," Billy assures me. "But if you don't want it, don't take it. You will find something else, Axe. You are great at what you do."

"Thanks." I smile. Hearing Billy say it makes me feel lighter. I can, and I will, turn down the position. I have the condo sale money to float on if I don't find a position right away. I'll be okay.

Billy stands up. "That's it? No meltdown about how I just told you that Gabriel loves you and is perfect for you and you should fight like hell for him because putting yourself out there this time will actually be worth it?"

I stand up too. "Well, actually you didn't say that last part until now. And so yeah, that freaks me out a little bit. I've always been shit with judgment when it comes to men."

"I'm not asking you to follow your judgment, Axe. I'm telling you to follow mine," Billy announces and grins like the egomaniac he always pretends to be. "I'm never wrong."

"Oh you are wrong probably about four hundred times a day," I assure him. "But you aren't wrong about Gabe. I know that. I *am* going to fight for this. For him. I just... needed to know you were in my corner."

"Always. Bring it in." Billy grabs me in a bro-hug.

I laugh and push him away. "Be safe out there, asshole."

"I'll try." Billy smiles.

I head out of his room and the Mirabella paddock and walk halfway down the row to the Mayflower paddock. I'm not looking for Gabe. He's got practice. Now is not the time to profess my feelings. But I'm hoping to catch Louis. I find him in the corner of the cafeteria with Henri, both with lattes in their hands and glued to a laptop. Henri notices me first as I approach. He gives me a polite smile. "Hey, Axel. We were just finalizing the press release."

"What press release?" I ask even though I already know what press release.

"The one announcing your split," Henri says simply. "Don't worry, it's very standard. Amicable, friends, respect, all the good words are in there. Also, we are holding off on announcing your role at the UK office until maybe a month from now. Just so it doesn't look like it was a bribe or something."

"Yeah. About that..." I swallow. I was really hoping to do this privately with Louis but it is what it is. I take a deep breath and roll my thumb over my commitment band. "I am respectfully turning down the job in London. But please know I am very grateful for the opportunity."

Henri looks like he's been slapped. But when my eyes shift to Louis, he's smiling softly. Henri closes the laptop. "I'm confused."

"It's a dream job, but honestly, I don't want a reward for being with Gabriel. Because I wasn't faking it. It wasn't some job. I fell in love with him and I just... I mean I don't know what is going to happen with us, maybe nothing. But I just don't want the job this way. So thank you. But I am rejecting the position."

"Henri, can you give us a moment *s'il te plait*?" Louis says, still smiling, still looking just at me.

Henri picks up his laptop and walks away without a word.

Louis uses the toe of his expensive loafer to push the now vacant chair toward me. "Sit."

I sit. He leans forward, toward me. "It's not maybe nothing."

"Pardon?"

"What's going to happen between you. What's already happened. It's not nothing," Louis assures me. "I knew that before I saw that condom wrapper on the bedroom floor."

I explode in a flush, and Louis just smirks. "I'm glad you feel so strongly about my son, but you don't have to give up the job."

"It feels right."

"Okay, well, once you work this out, the two of you, I will help you find another job," Louis tells me. "I have contacts everywhere and I would be happy to refer you."

"Thank you."

He stands so I do too, and he shakes my hand and then pulls me close and kisses each of my cheeks. "I'm going to watch the practice in the garage. Would you like to join me?"

I shake my head. "No, I'm going to head back to the hotel and wait for him there."

We walk to the entrance of the cafeteria together. "That press release Henri is working on..."

"Nothing gets released without my sign-off. And I am not signing off," Louis assures me. "Not yet. I have faith in you two."

"Thank you. Again."

We step outside into the small lane where all the paddocks are lined up, with the track just a few hundred yards away and I change my mind. "I'll go with you."

When we get to the garage, the practice session has already started. They go out at different times. Without the stress of having to set times that count, the mood in the garage is chill. Gabe is already in his car when we get there. All I can see are his eyes since his visor is up, but they light up when he sees me. I give him a small wave and follow Louis over to a monitor.

It may be one of my last times here, so I'm not hiding in a corner. Adam, his lead mechanic, walks over as Gabe's car starts down the pit lane. He holds his hand out toward me, Gabe's ring is in between his thumb and forefinger.

"Gabriel asked me to give this to you." My heart seizes. "He said you should hold onto it while he's in the car. He doesn't want to get fined but he doesn't want to lose it either."

Oh. Thank God.

I take it and push it onto my other ring finger. It feels odd and a little tight, but I don't care. Louis hands me some head-phones. "You'll hear the radio talk with these."

I slip them on and we watch the monitor. Gabriel is on his fourth lap when something happens. I don't know what because it's so quick. One minute he's on the track, starting a curve, and the next, the car is a blur of red, white, and blue, gravel is flying everywhere, dust obscures the cameras, black lines scar the pavement, and there's a crash. He's in the wall. Literally. His front end wedged under a barricade plastered with a sponsor's logos.

Every cell in my body seizes. My blood grows cold and it feels like all the oxygen has left earth. My lungs are empty. A voice on the radio echoes in my ears.

"Are you alright? Allard?"

It's seconds. Two. Maybe three. But they are the longest moments of my life. They feel like hours.

"Yeah. Fine. Sorry. I completely misread the turn. Sorry."

He sounds like he tapped a bumper in a parking lot, not like he smoked a wall at over a hundred kilometers an hour. I steal a glance at Louis. His mouth is set in a grim line, but he's breathing evenly. He looks up at me. "I'd like to say you get used to it, but you don't. However, you learn to live with it."

Oh my God, this is not going to be easy. Luckily I already know it's worth it.

HE'S FINE. I know this. I saw him get out of the car all by himself, without a problem. He took off his helmet and hopped on the back of a scooter and even waved to fans as they passed by the stands. He is perfectly fine. But it's not until he steps into the garage that my blood starts circulating and my heart starts beating again, I swear.

And all I want to do is rush over to him and hug him, feel that he's okay with my own hands, but I can't. I know that and I'm able to control my ridiculous, lovesick urges. He's out for the rest of practice now. They'll need to work on his car all night to get it ready for qualifying. Bob seems annoyed, Gabe seems disappointed, but all is well. This is normal, right? God this sport scares the shit out of me.

Finally, he makes his way to me. His dad squeezes his shoulder and leaves without a word. Gabe looks up at me. "Hey. I'm glad you came. Sorry, I didn't exactly give you much to watch."

"Oh you gave me a lot to watch," I reply and fight the urge to touch him. Not here. Not now. "Nothing I enjoyed. Or want to see again. But yeah, it was something."

Gabriel smiles. It's cheeky and heated. "Awe, honey, were you worried about me?"

"Damn fucking right."

We both let out huffs of laughter or maybe it's just tension. Who knows? He makes the move first, grabbing my right hand. He stares at his ring there, and with his other hand, he gently tugs it off. "I've gotta go do press so I'll take it back now if that's okay. Thanks for looking after it."

"Sure. I thought when Adam brought it to me that you... were giving it back," I admit, my voice a little husky.

Gabriel shakes his head, sandy hair skimming his forehead. "No. We're not there. I don't know where we are but it's not there."

"Good." I smile and a small flicker of hope illuminates my heart. "I'll wait for you at the hotel."

He nods. "See you soon."

I make all these plans while I'm being driven back to the hotel. What I'll order from room service for him. What I'll change into. How I will stand and most importantly what I will say. I even write down a couple of notes in my phone. A short, sweet to-do list on how to profess my undying love.

But then I get to the hotel and stride across the lobby and before I can get into the elevator, the whole plan goes to shit. Because someone calls out my name. "Axel! There you are!"

My sister is in front of me, walking towards me with her arms extended. "Cordy. What the hell are you doing here?"

"I told you I had a second piece of good news," she replies as she wraps me in a big hug. She smells like expensive perfume and flowery shampoo. "But you never bothered to ask what it was. Well, surprise! It's me coming to visit. And thanks so much for the warm welcome."

"I'm a shit," I admit and reach down to hug her again. I love Cordy and she has no idea what a complete clusterfuck my life has become, or that she's stepping into the middle of it in her fancy high heels. "I'm surprised but of course I'm happy to see you. I love seeing you."

"I miss having you right around the corner," Cordy tells me as our second hug breaks apart and she rubs the sides of my arms lovingly. "I mean sure I hardly ever saw you even when you did live there."

"Unless you had a Prosecco emergency," I note. My sister is the only person I know who will pop by unannounced, in a complete panic, begging to borrow a bottle of wine instead of a cup of sugar.

"I don't have those anymore. Did you know they deliver wine?" She smiles like she just discovered electricity. "But I still miss you. And worry. So I'm here. Also, I hear F1 drivers are hot. Are any single? Or straight?"

I smirk at her. "A few."

"Is yours single?" she asks and my gaze grows pointed. "Not for me. Ew. Gross. I don't do my bro's sloppy seconds. I mean... I heard his legal issue was cleared up. He's racing better than ever. Are you still... working for him?"

"I was never working for him. I was working for..." I sigh and pull her toward the elevators. I still have a plan I want to execute before Gabriel gets back from the track. I work best with a plan. "I have real feelings for him. And he has them for me. We're... trying to sort through it, which is why although I love seeing you, the timing sucks."

She takes that all in, furrowing her dark, straight eyebrows and puckering her mouth which is nice and full without the help of additives. She gets that from Mom, whose nickname is

Rosebud due to her full, puckered mouth. It was given to her by the bassist of a rock band when she was seventeen. It's a famous band I've purposely blocked out to avoid trauma. Your mother's mouth being named by a rock star is definitely therapy fodder. "I need to meet him. I need to run him through my bullshit filter, Axe. Yours is defective."

I roll my eyes. "You'll meet him. How about tonight? We could do a late dinner at the hotel restaurant?"

I am fucking with my plan, but the situation requires it. And besides, I kind of like the idea of Gabriel meeting someone in my family. Cordy is the best one to start with. There's baggage with my mom and an elephant in the room with my dad. "Dinner is good."

I kiss the top of her head and step into the elevator alone. I'll be able to get a little time alone with Gabe before dinner, and I can profess my true feelings then. So maybe when he meets my sister it will officially be as the man who knows I love him, not the fake boyfriend I may or may not be really dating.

As the doors begin to close she waves and announces, "I'll pop over to the restaurant and make the reservation. For five. Did I mention Mom and Dad are here? Toodles!"

Did she just...

What? No. Fuck.

I DON'T KNOW what I'm expecting when I finally make it back to the hotel. But I can tell you if I had to bet my career on it, I wouldn't have put my chips on 'meeting Axel's entire family'. I am exhausted and achy as hell, thanks to being slammed into a barrier at one-hundred and fifty-two kilometers. The car needs work, so everyone is pissed. It's funny when Samuels hits a wall, which he has done more than me this year, no one makes him feel like shit. When I do it, they act like it's on purpose.

All I want as the doorman holds the door to the hotel ajar for me, is to take a long shower, eat something, and finish the night with a massage because I convinced Enzo to come to the hotel and work on my back. I can't afford to be stiff in the qualifying tomorrow. Of course, I also want to see Axel and talk through what, exactly, our next steps are. But I'm feeling somewhat confident about the fact that there is an 'our' and that feels good. I've never been in love before so I don't know how to tell him, or even when. Is it too soon? I know Axel has had more relationships than me. And longer ones too. But the last one he was in sounds like it was shit. I don't want to do this wrong and hurt him. Or me. For the first time in my life, I care about my feelings. Because I have them.

I'm barely in the door to the hotel room when he walks right over to me. He's got his arms out like he's going to reach for me, but then he drops them and stops abruptly about a foot away. "How are you feeling? Everything must be sore."

"Yeah. Everything is," I admit and roll my neck. But then I lift both my arms, stretch them above my head, and watch as his gaze slips to the patch of exposed skin between my team shirt and my black pants. I smile and drop my hands on his shoulders, pulling him into me. "But this makes it feel better."

I nuzzle his neck, a glutton for the scent of him and the feel of him. His hands slide up my back, pressing me closer to him. I feel his lips touch my head and his breath rustle my hair.

"We need to talk." He says it with such seriousness that my stomach bottoms out. I rear back a little to look at him. "I did *not* invite them but... my family is here."

My head juts back farther and my arms slide from his shoulders. "Here? In France?"

"Worse. In this hotel." Axel looks so pained. He rubs the back of his neck and bites his bottom lip a moment and exhales. "And I have to meet them for dinner. And at first, I thought you should come. But now..."

"You don't want me there?"

"No. I always want you there, Gabe. I want you everywhere," Axel blurts out. He bites his lip again. "I didn't realize you'd be so long at the track. I thought we could talk first. And also, I can imagine you just want to relax after the day you've had, and my family... they aren't exactly Zen. My sister is a well-meaning wrecking ball, my mom is a hippie with a capital dippie, and my dad and I... our relationship is currently strained. Slightly. So—"

"So give me ten minutes to shower and change."

His eyelashes flutter in confusion. "Did you hear anything I just said?"

"I heard it all," I reply, pulling my shirt over my head and trying not to groan at the new, unwelcome tightness between my shoulders. "I need us to have a heart-to-heart too, but I'm not going to leave you hanging with your family. I have a feeling they've all seen the news stories and even if they know they're fake... I mean, that it was supposed to be fake, I think they should get to know me. Because we aren't faking it now, right?"

"No. We aren't." Axel's dark eyes somehow get darker, and he presses a hand to my chest, right above my heart. I cover that hand with one of my own. "Gabriel, I'm falling—"

I kiss him. Hard and fierce, my tongue purposely blocking any more words he might try to form. His hand curls, nails pressing into my skin with a delicious ache. And then I pull back. Because if I don't, we will never make it to dinner. Hell, I might not even make it to qualifying tomorrow. "Do not finish that sentence until we have the time to back those words up with actions, okay?"

He nods shakily.

Fourteen minutes later we walk across the hotel lobby toward the fancy French restaurant on the other side with our fingers laced together. "Just so I know what I'm getting into, they know you're gay?"

"Since I was sixteen."

"And nobody is uncomfortable with it?"

"Are you kidding? My mother acted like she won the lottery." Axel chuckles, his mouth tipping up in a grin that's whimsical and not a common feature for him. "She's a rock groupie, liberal, free-love, flower child. Having a gay kid gives her street cred. And my dad is bi."

"Really?" I don't know why that shocks me.

Axel nods. "Oh yeah. I mean, he's madly in love with my

mom but before my mom, he was dating a screenwriter named Micah. And before that an actress. And before that an actor. He didn't even blink when I came out."

"Cool." I have heard so many horror stories for gay kids coming out to their families. I'm glad Axel didn't live one.

We enter the restaurant and before the host can bring us to the table, a girl with long dark hair and dark eyes just like Axel's pops up from a round table by the window. She waves, blood-red nails flashing, and a smile much less inhibited than Axel's normal smile is plastered on her pretty face. Axel takes a breath and seems to hold it as he guides me toward her.

"Hi! I'm Cordelia. Or Cordy if you're family. Or Delia if it's work. You must be my new brother-in-law!" she chirps and pushes Axel to the side so she can hug me.

I chuckle and hug her back. "Technically it was a commitment ceremony and not a legal marriage. The media keep getting it wrong."

"Well, whatever it was, giving your parents a heads up Axel Jericho Maximus Walsh Hemming, would have been a good idea," a woman from the other side of the table says. With the same dark hair and high cheekbones, but much lighter eyes and slightly darker skin, she must be his mother. She's gorgeous and elegant in a bohemian way. She stands and levels those piercing eyes at me. "I was so flipped out I couldn't meditate for a week."

"I'm sorry for the anxiety, and lack of meditation," I say before Axel can apologize. I reach across the table with my hand. "I'm Gabriel. Nice to meet you."

"I know who you are. You're gorgeous and naughty. My two favorite things."

"Mom!" Axel groans.

"Yes, Rosebud, love. Don't scare the man," Dominic Hemming stands up and now I'm shaking his hand. He's a very tall, very fit man with Axel's pale complexion and dimpled chin.

He smiles at me and it's as reserved and guarded as his son's. "Let's sit and order. I'm fighting a losing battle with jet lag and I'm sure Gabriel has to have an early night."

I nod and Axel and I sit. The meal goes really well. Axel wasn't kidding, his family is a lot but for me, it's a bit of a dream. I grew up alone. An only child with one parent. My dad only had one sibling, a brother who disowned him when he came out as gay. My grandparents died before I was born so this larger, tight-knit family is fascinating and attractive. By the time we're enjoying coffees, I'm exhausted but glad I made the sacrifice and came. Especially when his dad mentions Eric and Axel's hand, which I have been holding under the table, goes limp.

"Dom, honey, not now." Rosebud, who has admitted her real name is Sharon but she hasn't used it since she was seventeen, shoots her husband a glare that only a wife can pull off.

And like a long-married husband, he ignores it. "I want to formally apologize for hiring that twat, Axel."

I squeeze his hand because Axel isn't saying anything. He also isn't looking at me, or anything but the remnants of his cappuccino. "I take it, it didn't work out?"

"No. The bastard charged me half a million and then didn't deliver any real traction," Dominic rants. "A couple of blog interviews with the stars. And some Facebook ads, where he spelled the name of the movie wrong. Sure he fixed it as soon as I called him screaming but—"

"You shouldn't have to tell a public relations firm how to spell the name of the movie," Axel interjects, sounding annoyed.

"Anyway, I am suing him. But in the meantime I need someone to stop the bleeding," Dominic tells his son. "The festival circuit is coming up. I need to get this film into Cannes, but with no buzz, I don't see that happening."

"I have a few names I can call who might be able to work with you," Axel says.

Cordy flicks her brother with her napkin. "He wants you to work with him you dopey koala!"

"Me? No."

"Why? Do you have another job?" Dominic demands.

Axel's eyes flash to me. Finally. He looks so absurdly uncomfortable. And then he drops my hand, which he was barely holding anyway, and pushes his chair back. "You're right. Gabe has to rest for tomorrow and I'm sure your jetlag is all-consuming at this point. Let's pick this up in the morning."

"Sure. That should give you some more time to figure out how to avoid working with me," Dominic snaps, and I'm suddenly wondering what the hell I'm missing and then Axel stands up.

"Avoid working with you? You didn't ask me to work with you. You just hired my ex and never even told me. I had to read about it in Variety," Axel retorts heatedly.

"You told me years ago that you didn't want our businesses intertwined."

"That was when I had a business."

"Okay. Let's pick this up tomorrow," Rosebud says, her voice light but she's definitely not suggesting, she's demanding. She reaches into her purse, which I notice is an Allard bag, and walks around the table and drops a crystal into Axel's hand.

"Solidite for calmness and clarity." She turns to me and drops one into the center of my palm. "Agate for healing. You've been rolling your shoulders all night."

She hugs Axel and he hugs her back. "Love you, my boy. I'm going to stick rose quartz under your dad's pillow tonight. You know how that calms him."

We say goodbye to Cordy and Dominic, although that goodbye is frosty between him and his son. We don't speak until we get to the room. I am the one to break the ice. "He hired your ex?"

"Yep."

"For public relations?"

"Yep."

"Your ex worked in the same field as you?"

"Yep."

Well, this isn't a very two-sided conversation. I roll my shoulders again and pull out the crystal Rosebud gave me and put it on the bar. "Can you say something other than yep?"

"Yep. Sure."

He's pacing by the window, eyes down on the fancy lush carpet. I lean against the bar. "Want me to suck you off?"

"Ye— what? No. I mean, what the fuck?"

I smile because I finally got him to look at me. And although something in his expression holds shame and pain, he's still fucking gorgeous to me. "I'm just trying to get you to talk to me. You sometimes let out a whole lot of words when you come."

"I don't want to talk about this. Or think about it. Or tell you what a total idiot I've been," Axel mutters. "I spent years changing people's images, rebranding them. Seeing them for exactly who they were but making sure the world saw something better. And I didn't know that I wasn't seeing my partner for who he was."

"We all make mistakes," I say simply.

"He's the reason I don't have a company of my own anymore," Axel says and stops pacing. He runs his hand through his hair and stares at the carpet again. "He worked for me. We were already dating, as you know. We were in a good place when we got back together after my New Year's in Monaco. I thought. And he was a good accounts manager at his other firm. So I thought sure. I was careful and filled out paperwork with my own HR department so it was on-record we had an out-of-office relationship. But I didn't make him sign a non-compete because he was supposed to love me. We were supposed to trust each other. That's what he told me when I brought it up. So I dropped it."

I shake my head, not at Axel's mistake. But he misinterprets me. He turns to the window and tugs on his hair. "I know. I'm a fool. A loser. I've always had shit taste in men and no self-preservation."

Ouch. I struggle not to take that personally because I am a man he picked. I walk up behind him and grab his shoulders. He's tense and he tries to step away but I don't let him. "I am not judging you in the least, Axe. I am very happy that you were stupid enough to give me a real shot."

He smiles at that, but it's fleeting. I wrap my arms around him from behind. He reaches up and wraps a hand around my forearm, where it's wrapped around his chest. "I didn't mean you. You aren't a mistake."

"I know," I whisper against the back of his ear. The French countryside rolls out in front of us, dark and looming. "I don't believe in mistakes. If Eric hadn't screwed you over, and you hadn't closed your agency, you wouldn't have been hired by my dad. And we never would have met again. And I never would have almost heard you tell me you love me."

Slowly, Axel turns in my arms. His eyes are wide and his cheeks rosy. It's my favorite Axel. The one who is scared shitless but not about to back down. "You told me not to tell you."

"Lay it on me now. I can handle it," I say in my best tough American guy voice.

Axel laughs. "Well, now I'm not sure I want to."

I laugh too and pull him closer, sliding my hands down to cup his ass. I pull him into me and feel our cocks stir at the same time. "Okay well, keep the words in that pretty little mouth of yours and show me instead."

"Good idea." He pauses to kiss me long and slow. "Anyone

can say anything, whether it's true or not. But a cock in the ass, that speaks louder than words."

I laugh. Scratch that, I think as we start to undress each other. My favorite Axel is this one. The one with the dirty words and hard dick. The one who wants me despite all his many sensible thoughts. I cuff the back of his neck when we're naked so that I can hold our mouths together while our bodies touch. We find the bed. He tumbles onto it first and everything is like it always is between us—passionate and needy and real.

But I roll him over, so he's on top of me and I'm under him, his legs between mine, our cocks leaking as they grapple for space between us. I run my fingertips over his cheeks and into his hair as he whispers, "You want me on top?"

I give him the answer I've been thinking about forever. "I want you inside me."

I don't ask Gabriel if he's bottomed before. I assume he has. He is someone who is not afraid to be sexually curious. Unlike me. And I wonder if I should tell him I've never topped before. Then again, I never bothered to mention that my entire sexual history is four guys, including him, so I guess I don't need to mention this. Instead, when he's ready after I rim him and my lube-covered fingers have him open and panting, I roll on a condom and I slowly and steadily work my way inside.

This feels even better than I thought it would, and I thought it would be incredible. I sweat with the restraint it takes not to grab his slim hips and tug him down until he's impaled on my cock. But I know what he's feeling. The stretch, the burn, the struggle to let go and search out the pleasure hiding in the pain. If you don't hunt it down, you won't find it. It doesn't come to you. As I push deeper, another ring of muscle pulsing over my shaft, I realize, as a top, I'm the hunted. My orgasm is actively chasing me, and it's going to catch me. So when he grips my trembling forearm and presses his eyes shut and gasps out, "Wait," I'm more than happy to.

I watch him regulate his breathing, and when I kiss the

strong neck of his I feel his pulse hammering beneath my lips. He lifts a hand and drops it on the back of my neck, fingers tousling the ends of my hair. "I love you."

"Not as long or as hard as I love you, *mon amour*," he whispers back.

"I think I'm pretty long and hard," I say, surprising myself. He brings out the absolute devil in me and it's scary how much I like it.

Gabriel licks the column of my neck, biting down just above my collarbone. "Prove it."

I move again. And suddenly, I'm all the way in. I've shared my body with him countless times now, but sharing his body... it's magic. My rhythm is chaotic, his hips buck and his back arches like he lives for this chaos so no complaints are coming from the perfect man under me, just moans and French swear words. Or maybe prayer words...

His hand is wrapped around his cock and he's tugging hard, eyes closed, mouth open, and I whisper every indecent thing I can think of in his ear. Every dirty thought I've ever had about him. Every sexual act we've yet to explore but is on my list. *Our* list...

"I'm not going to last," I confess, humiliated.

"I like it fast, baby. Fast is what I do for a living," he reminds me, but I barely hear it. I'm coming so hard I whimper.

I don't waste time. I refuse to allow myself to enjoy an orgasm he didn't have with me. So I pull out and he starts to complain until I slide lower and take his dick, heavy, hard, and vibrating with need, into my mouth. He comes down the back of my throat moments later. We fall asleep almost immediately, sweaty and dirty and completely satiated.

When I wake the sun is a light glow across the corner of the room. My phone, which is on the night table by the condom wrapper, says six. Gabriel stirs beside me, rolling onto his back. I roll onto my side, facing him, and stare. Did we make it through? Is it really that simple? Am I finally lucky?

After a few minutes, he opens one eye and lets out a soft groan. "It's early. Sleep."

"I need to tell you I turned down the job in London," I whisper, like if I say it quietly, it will make less of an impact. But this is a big deal, and now both his midnight blue eyes are open. He rolls to face me too, tucking an arm under the pillow.

"So what are you going to do about work?"

"Find something else."

He studies me, reaches out, and runs his fingers behind my ear like he's tucking away hair that isn't there. "Your dad has something else."

"Gabe..."

"Hear me out, okay?" he begs, and I sigh but nod and bite my bottom lip to keep from interrupting. "I'm not saying forever. I'm just saying help him out of this jam. Clean up your asshole ex's mess. It will make you feel powerful, and your dad not only needs you, he wants you. Do it. And then come back to me, immediately, and finish out the season with me. There are only two races left. You could get back in time for Singapore, the last one. And then we can vacation together again. And we'll find you a job together. I'll help."

He looks at me, hopeful, vulnerable, and actually worried that I might say no. I can't. I'm that pushover romantic who will do just about anything my lover asks of me. Luckily this time I picked a lover who looks out for my heart like he does his own. So I nod and sigh. "Fine. I'll do it. It will be some nice money, and a chance to bond with my dad."

"You're going to charge him?"

"Double," I say and we both laugh.

• • •

I leave the next day before qualifying. Before the race. I hate it because Gabe was achy this morning, and not just from me. His shoulders are stiff from the crash and he canceled a massage for my family dinner so I worry about him the whole flight to Los Angeles, which is stupidly long.

And now we have a time difference between us. Nine entire hours so it makes keeping in touch a chore. But one we both gladly go out of our way to make happen. Los Angeles is a lot of meetings and some contracts. I set up my dad's indie film with a social media team and use every contact I've ever had to book him a bunch of television interviews and even more print, all over the world. We spend the nights together. While Gabriel is already asleep across the world, Dad and I talk and joke and by the end of the week together I feel like any rift between us is gone. He hugs me goodbye at the airport. He's on a flight back to Australia and I'm making the long haul to Singapore. If my flights go just right, I will get there before the race starts.

"Thank you for everything, Axe. I should have listened to you from the beginning. Even if you couldn't help, I shouldn't have used that fucker," my dad says, hugging me tightly. "I love you. And I really like this French kid. Because I can tell he really likes you."

"Thanks, Dad. It's my fault. I should have helped you. I got hung up on making my own name. I shouldn't have. And if you need me again, I'm here," I promise. "And it means a lot that you like Gabe because he's going to be around a lot. And for a long time."

I kiss his cheek, something I haven't done since I was a little boy, and he rubs it in like he used to do to delight me when I was six. Then I'm rushing to get to my first gate and start this trip. I haven't heard Gabriel's voice in two days. He's in Singapore now and the time difference is a staggering fifteen hours so we survive on text messages that pop in at all hours of the day and night.

The flights should take nineteen hours and then there's an hour-long drive to the track. But weather fucks my connection in San Francisco and I'm delayed two hours. When I get to the airport in Singapore, I can't find the car I ordered. And my bag never makes it off the carousel. I decide to deal with it later and not even inform the airline help desk, which has a line fourteen people long. I make my way out of the airport into the thick Singapore air and pay a taxi cab double the normal rate to get me to the track. It's a city track so the closest he can get, with all the security zones and road closures, is five blocks away. I have to haul ass the rest of the way by foot and by the time I get to the private security gate, I feel, and probably look, like a wool sock left on a clothesline in a hurricane. Wet, droopy, and smelly.

Henri is there, just like Louis promised, with a VIP pass for me. "They're on lap fifty of sixty-one. Hurry!" Henri says and we start to jog. "Gabriel is in third."

"Third?" I echo and fuck the jogging, I am full-out running now.

He didn't have a great race in France. They fixed the car, but he ended up with a grid penalty because of new parts and started second from last. The track wasn't great for passing opportunities, so he floundered toward the bottom of the pack the whole race, ending up sixteenth. I know it doesn't matter. He's had a solid season without it. Other rookies have definitely done worse. But I want him to have some points this season. A podium, well that would be more than even I dare to ask of the Universe. But points... sitting in third means he has a long way to fall to miss points. He won't. I know it. He won't miss points this time.

Louis looks a little aghast when he sees my condition when I arrive at the garage. Henri broke off to go to the paddock. He hands me some headphones and whips his handkerchief out of the front pocket of his tailored blazer and hands it to me. I pat myself down, eyes glued to the race. Gabriel is doing amazing. In front of him is Grady Lewis and Cristian Rivera. Behind him, and I mean right up his ass, is Billy James. They come out of a turn, into a straightaway, and Billy immediately tries to overtake Gabe. I'm clenching my fists and holding my breath. If they collide, which happens a lot, it will kill both of them.

Their battle is "epic" according to Adam, who brings me a water. But when we're on the final lap, the battle causes Billy to lock up, and he nearly slides off the track but regains control. Still, he gets passed by Nord, who doesn't gain enough speed to challenge Gabriel before the checkered flag is waving.

Louis lets out a roar and I scream at the top of my lungs and bear hug him. Adam is jumping up and down like a trampolinist beside us. Pablo is a foot away grinning despite himself. Into the comms he announces, "Gabriel Allard you are P3. P3. Your first points and podium. What is it they say in your country? *Magnifique!*"

Gabriel lets out a hoot and a bunch of French words they'll probably have to bleep on television. "Yes. Thank you, Mayflower. Thank you, Adam and my dad. And my boyfriend, wherever you are. Thank you all. This is... *c'est une reve.* A dream."

Louis yanks off his headphones, and I pull mine off and we grab Adam and run to the place where the top three cars park before the trophy ceremony. I'm shocked to see the entire team waiting to congratulate him as he pulls himself out of the car. He stands on it, pumps a fist into the air, and people cheer. And then, he jumps down, lifts his visor, and rushes the Mayflower team. They lift him off the ground. Good. He deserves their praise. Finally.

Louis leans over to me. "He has an offer from another team for next season."

I shoot him a wide-eyed stare and he lifts his hands. "I have nothing to do with it," he promises. "This one is all him. And I am staying out of it. But let him talk it through with you."

I nod. "I'll always be there for him."

Louis smiles and nods.

"You made it!" Gabriel's voice calls out in awe. He's still standing with his team but he sees me and his dad at the back of the crowd. People part for us and we move forward as he yanks off his helmet and wraps his arms around both of us and we hug him.

And then, before he rushes off to get weighed and do press and get his first F1 trophy, he leans over, grabs my face in his hands, and kisses me. Cameras flash, people cheer, and he slips me the goddamn tongue. I laugh and step back. "You..." I laugh, turning red.

He winks at me and walks away.

He may be the one about to collect a trophy, but I'm the one who is the real winner here. At least, it feels that way.

I FEEL ALL the things I'm supposed to feel watching my son stand on the podium for his first win in the ultimate league of his chosen sport. Pride, joy, excitement. But I feel a couple things that might not be as normal. Relief. Sadness. Relief that he's done it. Gabriel could never be a failure to me. I wouldn't care if he finishes every race last as long as he's happy. But I know he wanted this and he worked for it, despite what people think. I'm also sad because... well, he's done it on his own.

I've been an overbearing parent his whole life. I see that now. And Gabriel has let me. I don't think, looking back, it benefited either of us and though I've tried to step back and let him make his own way in recent weeks, it isn't easy. I miss being the one person he relied on.

Beside me, Axel beams up at Gabriel who is walking to the little round platform for the third place winner. Thankfully most of the Mayflower crew is there behind us, cheering and clapping. They didn't need to be told to come and support their driver. I would have demanded it if I had to, and Axel would have been right there with me, I know. He's a great young man. I didn't think there would be a real connection when I hired him.

It was honestly the furthest thing from my mind, which seems stupid now.

It's not that I didn't want Gabriel to find someone to love. I've just never really done it myself, so I assumed he inherited my inability to settle down. And don't get me wrong, my life is full. Even before I decided to have Gabriel I had a full life, so the one thing I never meddled with was Gabriel's romantic life. If he had one partner or a different one every month it didn't bother me, as long as he was happy. And Gabriel had *seemed* happy. Now, with Axel, I know without a shadow of a doubt that he is.

A woman in a formal dress walks in front of the podium and gives Gabriel his trophy. He lifts it high in the air and Axel whistles so loudly I may be deaf in my left ear now. Bob is beside me and he winces.

"It's third," Bob says quietly, with a scowl.

"It's a podium, as a rookie, with basically no help from his team, a-k-a you," Axel clarifies. "So yeah. I'm gonna cheer the hell out of my man."

I grin. Bob huffs in disgust and walks away. Axel is a little pink as he looks at me. "Sorry. I just…"

"Don't apologize," I shush him. "That was glorious."

Axel laughs and I pat his back. I would ruffle his hair like I do Gabriel but he's too damn tall. We turn back to the scene in front of us as the other two drivers get their trophies. Grady Lewis from Arete finished second and, not surprisingly, Cristian Rivera easily took first.

And then it hits me, as the Spanish national anthem is played, for the winner, all three men on this podium are LGBT. "*Mon dieu, le chemin parcouru…*"

Axel looks at me inquisitively. "I think I should take French classes over the break."

I chuckle. "I basically said Oh God, how far have we come."

Now he looks a little more confused so I elaborate. "The three men up there are all not straight. In a major world sport. It may be a first."

Axel looks awed. "That's freaking cool."

"I agree," I know I've promised myself I would take a step back in Gabriel's life, now that his name has been cleared, but I can't stop myself from asking Axel about their next steps. "Are you two coming back to Paris for winter break?"

"We haven't discussed it actually," Axel admits and gives me a small smile. "But I'd definitely be up for it. I think I'm going to try and grab some freelance jobs here and there so I may not be there the whole time."

Gabriel is grabbing the champagne now and I know what happens next. All three drivers shake the bottles and begin to spray each other. Then my wild son turns to the crowd and sprays us. Because he wouldn't be my beautiful brash son if he didn't take everything just one step farther than most. And as sticky booze rains down over us, Axel tips his head back, opening his mouth to catch it.

As the celebration simmers down, Axel and I start to make our way around the corner of the stage to meet up with Gabriel. Someone touches my shoulder and I turn and am suddenly shaking the hand of Michael Meeks. He's the owner of Apex, another team on the grid. "Your son has had a healthy season for a rookie. Congrats."

"Thanks. I'm thrilled with his performance too," I say, wondering why he's talking to me now when he's never done more than a polite nod or passing hello.

Michael leans in and drops his voice. "Are you his manager? Gabriel's?"

Oh. I see... I shake my head. "I know a lot of people think I am but he actually has a proper one."

I pull a card out of my pocket and slip it to him, glancing around to make sure no one notices. Michael tucks it into his pocket and smiles gratefully. "I'm hoping we can offer Gabriel—."

"As an investor in Mayflower, I'm going to stop you right there," I want to yell yes! Yes you can! This team has better cars and a very bright future compared to Mayflower, but it's not my place. "My son's involvement is separate from my investment though so... use the card."

Michael nods. He gets it. He thanks me and keeps moving in the opposite direction through the crowd. Axel has moved on ahead, and I find him by the side of the stage, wrapped in an embrace and a not-safe-for-work kiss with my son. "You two want to dial it back to PG-13 *s'il te plait.*"

Gabriel pulls back from Axel, keeping his arm draped around his shoulder. I notice he's taken off that tin band he has been wearing since his fake commitment ceremony which everyone is still calling a marriage. I still think pieces of my heart are in my loafers, where they plummeted when I woke up to the headlines. I will give Gabriel his space but not when it comes to his wedding. Whenever that may be, and I'm fairly certain it's visible on the horizon, it's going to be lavish, and public, and big and I will most definitely be there. Crying into a designer handkerchief.

"I need a shower. Champagne is sticky," Gabriel announces as we walk back to the paddock.

"Get used to it, babe," Axel says, grinning. "There's more wins coming your way next season, I know it."

"I hope so," my son replies.

I look up at him and swell with pride as I tell him. "Apex will be contacting your manager. They're interested."

"Apex? Are you sure?" Gabriel stage whispers back at me,

his blue eyes, a feature he inherited from his mother, according to the egg donors fact sheet, are wide. "That's two teams."

"Probably more before the break ends. Your contract is up next year and no one wants to wait until the last minute," I remind him. "You're hot."

"Yes he is," Axel mutters and I glance up at him and he turns red. "Sorry. You weren't supposed to hear that."

I laugh and Axel gets redder, which I wouldn't have thought possible. "Oh, and you should expect a call from the director of F1."

"Me? Why?" Axel looks petrified.

"Holly, their Communication Head, is going on maternity leave next year," I explain. "It's a one-year replacement contract. I took the liberty of submitting the resume you gave Allard Couture. Oh, and a reference letter as a Mayflower sponsor."

Gabriel laughs. "I think the only work you actually did for the team was yell at me in a sauna to play nice with the media."

"So you aren't mad I interfered? Again?" I ask Gabriel who isn't shooting me death stare like I feared he might. Axel doesn't look mad either, just kind of confused.

Gabriel shakes his head and his eyes soften. "I really appreciate you trying to help Axe out, dad. Thank you."

"Yes, thank you," Axel parrots with a grateful smile.

"Well, I have two sons to meddle with now. It's a lot of work, but I happily accept the challenge," I joke and look down paddock row trying and concentrate on the containers painted in the various team colors. If I focus on my boys I'm likely to tear up and I'll be mortified.

I'm just so grateful I was right. Axel Walsh was the light at the end of the tunnel.

For the love story of Jasper Nord and Cristian Rivera, the Swedish prince/F1 driver and his sexy Spanish rival, read Off Track by Leslie McAdam. For the age gap romance of Ben Carpenter and Grady Lewis, the grizzled crew chief and the hotshot rookie, read Close Quarters by Regina Kyle.

ACKNOWLEDGMENTS

First, a huge thank you to Leslie McAdam and Regina Kyle for creating the Faster series with me. I loved every minute of working with you both!

Thanks to my family, especially my husband Jack and my mom. Big shout out of gratitude to my editor Brandi for being so flexible when Covid sidelined me. Thanks Mignon at Oh So Novel for the amazing covers! Also thanks to J.E. Birk, Laurel Greer, Kat Mizera, Lex Martin, Sarina Bowen, Hope Irving and the other authors who have supported me through this crazy career. Thanks to the 64 Players, who give me a reason to step away from the keyboard every now and then.

Thank you Kimberly and Brower Literary for your ongoing support and guidance. To you, the reader who dived into our Faster series, thank you, and I hope our boys ended up P1 in your hearts.

Victoria Denault is an award-winning Canadian author.

Her other M/M romances include:

Dauntless (Winner; Best Queer Romance, 2023 Canadian Romance Awards)

The Summer We Surrendered

Unwrapping the Truth (December 2023)

Her M/F sports romances include:

The Chase

Fast Track

Conner (January 2024)

Blindsided

Comets Christmas series

The San Francisco Thunder Series

Hometown Players series

More info at victoriadenault.com